The Diary of Young Arthur Conan Doyle

The Death of
Sherlock Holmes

I0628244

Edited

by

Dr. John Raffensperger
& Richard Krevolin

Paperback ISBN 978-1-78705-979-5
ePub ISBN 978-1-78705-980-1
PDF ISBN 978-1-78705-981-8

Published in the UK by MX Publishing
335 Princess Park Manor, Royal Drive,
London, N11 3GX
www.mxpublishing.co.uk

Covers painted by Ewa Czarniecka,
graphic design Kyra Dunn, compilation Brian Belanger.

To our esteemed editor, Nancy Cohen, our wonderful agent, Paula Munier, Renee Braeunig, Melanie Jappy, Kathy Copas, Colleen Sell, Dr. Wally Duff, Dr. Glenn Shepard, John Haslett, Penny Macleod, Steve Callender, Katja Bressette, Katia Haddidian, Coach Bob Orgovan, and the Sanibel writing group four.

EDITORS' NOTE

When an old trunk of Sir Arthur Conan Doyle's personal effects came up for auction at Sotheby's, we placed a bid and won the lot. Deep inside the rotting wooden chest, under his old medical instruments and clothes, was a series of hand-written journals. And, neatly tucked inside the first journal was this note:

"It is July 7, 1930. I am gravely ill and do not think I will live through the night. And so, it has become incumbent upon me to deal with these four leather-bound journals from my medical school days. I have always treasured them since they reveal the most personal details of the formative moments of my young life.

Due to their private nature, I thought it would be unseemly if they outlived me, so I walked them over to the fireplace in my library. However, as the heat of the flames licked their spines, I was unable to fully carry out my mission.

And so now, I reluctantly place these journals in this old footlocker and hope that these intimate entries are not exploited in a most untasteful way and instead, that one day, they are published in their entirety in order to convey to the world the simple truth about the grand adventures I had during my medical apprenticeship and the role played by Mr. Sherlock Holmes in developing my fictional detective.

-- Sir Arthur Conan Doyle"

And so, more than one hundred years
later, you now hold the third "lost
diary" of Sir Arthur Conan Doyle,
written while he was in practice at
Southsea. This volume details the true
story of Doyle's journey across the
American continent with Dr. Joseph
Bell to San Francisco and the role
played by Mr. Sherlock Holmes in
foiling a Russian plot to take back
Alaska.
. This diary provides further convincing evidence that Arthur
Conan Doyle based his fictional detective on a real Sherlock
Holmes.

-- The Editors: Dr. J. Raffensperger and Prof.
Richard Krevolin, 23 October, 2021

15 May 1883, Bush Villas, Southsea

I attended the butcher's epileptic fit until he was out of danger and left him with a packet of bromide powders. His wife paid with a pound of bacon and twenty pence. This afternoon, I opened the door at a knock only to see a one-horse gypsy caravan. I expected they were begging until I heard a piteous cry. It was a baby with pustules, a clear case of measles. I dabbed carbolic ointment on the sores and gave the poor mother a bottle of very dilute laudanum so the exhausted babe could sleep. They offered three pence, but I surmised that would leave them with nothing for food. I took their coppers and gave them the butcher's twenty pence.

A typical day . . . Earnings: a pound of bacon and three pence.

16 May 1883, Bush Villas, Southsea

I awoke to fierce banging on my door in the grey light of early dawn. I hurriedly put on a pair of trousers and ran downstairs. It was the constable, William Beade, whom I knew from the rugby club. He wore no hat, his clothing was disheveled, and there was a two-inch, bleeding gash on his forehead. "Come right in. You need stitches," said I.

"No, No, come immediately. Lady Stanhope has gone berserk again," said he. I snatched my medical bag and raced after the constable to the most fashionable part of Southsea. The Stanhope sisters were widows and definitely upper-class gentry. *My fortunes are taking a turn for the better*, I thought.

As we turned the corner, I heard screams interspersed with pitiable wails. "Have mercy! Oh, oh, the rats! The horrible rats! Get them off me!" Lady Stanhope, a woman of about sixty, was in the street, half-naked, with her back against a brick wall. Her eyes were wild, her hands trembled, and her disheveled, grey hair hung like coiled snakes over her bare shoulders. She flailed the air with a stout cane that was thick enough to disable a strong man.

"She hit me with the cane," said Constable Beade. A second constable darted close to the poor woman in an attempt to snatch the cane. She gave him a terrific smack on his right arm. He yelped with pain and retreated. It could have been bedlam, but this was one of our better neighborhoods, and the normally well-behaved Stanhope sisters were in the upper echelons of high society. My mind raced with the diagnostic possibilities. Could it be a brain tumor, an unusual stroke, or was she insane?

"Hold it, men. This calls for a change of tactics," said I. The poor woman trembled, cursed, and tried to remove the rest of her already-shredded night dress.

"Oh, get them off me! Oh, please!" she screamed. She beat the cobblestones with her cane and dragged her fingernails across her naked breasts, leaving trails of blood. The neighbors were out in force. Some offered suggestions and others demanded an end to the commotion. I then noticed on the doorsteps another woman, also in a nightdress.

4

"Are you the sister?" I asked. She dabbed her eyes with a soggy handkerchief.

"Yes, Lady Jane is my older sister," said she.

"When did this start?" I asked, aiming to retain my composure.

"Oh, the poor dear never went to bed, hasn't had a wink of sleep, but kept up all night long, walking and muttering to herself until she ran out to the street."

I was even more perplexed. The screaming stopped for a moment, then resumed, more intense than ever. "Help me God... The spiders!" Lady Stanhope had thrown down her cane and was tearing her hair with both hands, apparently in an attempt to remove what she imagined were spiders. Constable Beade quickly snatched up the cane, while the second constable managed to grab both of her arms. I hastily filled a syringe with a generous dose of morphine sulphate and jabbed the medicine into her arm. It should have been enough to subdue a strong man, but it had little or no effect; she managed to tear loose from the constables and fled down the street. Beade grabbed her with a flying tackle, and I administered a second dose of morphine. Lady Stanhope went limp, though continued to whimper piteously about spiders, rats, and a rabbit that she claimed was clawing her ankles.

We put her to bed and securely wrapped her in a sheet, but she continued to moan and, at times, cry out. Exhausted by the wild chase and chaos, I finally slumped into a chair before again addressing Lady Jane's sister.

"Has this happened before?" I asked.

"Oh yes. She has gone off like this twice in the past five years."

"How long do the spells last?"

"Three or four days or until Dr. Jones comes and prescribes for her." Jones was one of Southsea's most respected physicians who mainly looked after the upper-class gentry.

"What is the medicine?" I asked.

"That is the problem. She took two bottles on Friday, forgot to get more on Saturday, and the shops were closed yesterday. Perhaps I can find an empty bottle." She left and returned with a bottle on which a pink label, illustrated with a picture of a kindly lady, read: 'AUNT MARY'S FEMALE TONIC.' It was a six-ounce bottle, and at the bottom of the label, in fine print, it read: 'forty percent alcohol by volume.'

"Your sister is suffering from delirium tremens," said I. "This medicine is no different from whisky and she is in alcohol withdrawal."

"Well, I never heard of such a thing! This is medicine, not drink! How dare you suggest she is withdrawing from alcohol use? I shall call Dr. Jones. Young man, leave and never set foot in this house again!"

Later, I stitched Constable Beade's forehead where Mrs. Stanhope had hit him. "Thank ye, sir," said he. It is customary for physicians to treat the police and firemen for free. Thus, my day's efforts added nothing to my cash balance. Fortunately, I still had a half-pound of bacon.

I have been making more time for photography as of late. It is a fine way to view the world and often helps soothe any agitation, such as that I was feeling after my visit with the Stanhope sisters. So, I picked up my folding, bellows-body, half-plate camera, and a tripod, and went for a short stroll. After attempting to capture an image of the setting sun, and spending the time outdoors in great contemplation, I made two decisions about my life. The first is to qualify as a Doctor of Medicine, with the hope that the added degree will attract more patients. Secondly, I shall finally achieve the dream I have long held and write a novel of great deeds, derring-do with a bit of history. I shall begin in earnest by joining the Portsmouth Literary and Scientific Society and taking leave from the practice for just a few days. During that time, I plan to venture to Edinburgh where I can visit my family and further observe the source of inspiration for my novel's main character, my former professor at the Edinburgh Medical School, Dr. Joseph Bell.

20 May 1883, Edinburgh

When I arrived in Edinburgh, I left my bag with my mam and hurried so as not to miss Dr. Bell's afternoon clinic. I slipped into the third row in the great amphitheater, hoping to evade notice, but nothing escaped the observant professor, who witnessed my entrance and gave me a sly wink. Though relieved to no longer have to spend every day in lectures and labs, it was grand to be back in the old place with the familiar, lingering odor of chloroform and carbolic from the morning's surgery. The floor was swept clean except for a small heap of blood-stained sawdust beneath the operating table.

Dr. Bell's clerk — a callow, second-year student — stood like a dummy, thumbing through his notebook after he brought in his patient. I felt a pang of sympathy, having been in his place only a couple of years ago. The patient was a solidly-built fellow with streaks of grey in his reddish-brown beard and a fine Scottish face. He was dressed like a countryman in a clean, flannel shirt and faded, black and green plaid trousers, which were tucked into cowhide boots. He lurched when he walked and favored his left foot.

"Well, now, Mr. Weeks. Have ye lost your tongue? Please tell us the patient's history and your diagnosis," said the professor. The other students, cruel boys in their youth, howled and stomped their feet at their fellow student's misery. I recalled being in that same situation and felt pity for the poor clerk. If history shows anything, however, in a year or two, they will settle down to learn decorum and the proper business of our profession.

The poor clerk found his voice at last. "Sir, the patient is sixty years old and has a limp. I suspect he has a sprain."

"Is that all, Weeks?" Dr. Bell asked.

"Aye, sir..."

The professor ran his hand through his head of pure white hair and stood to his full height. With twinkling eyes, he pointed me out with a long, slender finger. "One of our recent distinguished graduates has granted us the favor of his presence. Mr. Conan Doyle, if you please, give us your diagnosis."

I was nonplussed and afraid the professor would embarrass me as he had done so many times in the past. Then, I spotted a tattoo — a faded anchor surrounded by a white circle — on the back of the patient's right hand. "Sir, the man was in the navy and, during his world travels, contracted syphilis. His lurching gate is due to *tabes dorsalis*," said I.

"It's a mistake yer a makin'. As a lad, I was in the volunteer lifeboat service at Arbroath. I ne'er been in the navy or left Scotland. The anchor and life ring tattoo is a badge of service," said the patient. A wide smile spread over his weather-beaten face.

Dr. Bell circled the patient, sniffed like a bird dog on a scent, sat down, extended his long legs, and folded his hands over his chest. "Now, Mr. Cameron, your cows are giving an abundance of milk?"

"Right, sir."

"You have lost almost two stone of weight in the past weeks."

"Nearer to three stone, sir."

"And you must get up at night to pass water?"

"Aye, I'm a spending most of me night at the pot."

"Mr. Weeks, kindly take your patient into the side room and secure a sample of urine," said Dr. Bell.

In a few moments, the clerk returned with the patient and a flask of urine.

"Now, observe carefully . . ." Dr. Bell said, as he squinted at the yellow liquid. He shook the flask until the urine foamed, then inserted his finger, brought the finger to his mouth and tasted the urine. There was no expression on his face, but the students cried out with astonishment. I was amazed at his performance. It was unusual, even for a showman like Dr. Bell. "Now lads, pass the jar and each of you sample the urine exactly as I demonstrated," he said. The flask went from student to student. Each carefully inserted a finger and, grimacing with disgust, tasted a sample. I took the tiniest drop on the tip of my tongue. It had a sweetish taste. I knew the diagnosis, but kept my peace and watched the students squirm.

Dr. Bell pointed to a chubby student in the first row. "What did you taste?" he asked.

"Sir, it was sweetish, like honey," said the student.

"You are quite correct. The diagnosis is diabetes mellitus. As you all know from your Latin, *mel* is the word for honey. I am sad, however, that not one of you noticed how I sampled the urine even though I asked you to do exactly as I had demonstrated. Remember, I have told you many times to observe every detail. Gentlemen, if you had paid close attention, you would have observed that I inserted my index finger into the urine but tasted my third finger."

The students groaned but wrote furiously in their notebooks.

"Gentlemen, you are about to see wet gangrene. Mr. Cameron, will you be so kind as to remove your boot?"

A foul odor rose in the cockpit when the patient removed his boot and sock. His foot was dusky blue in color, blistered, and dripped green pus.

"Mr. Cameron, I am indeed sorry, but there is no alternative to an amputation of your foot. My house officer will arrange a bed for you in the infirmary," the professor said in a soft, sad voice.

It was another of Dr. Bell's great triumphs of observation and diagnosis. The students were too shy to ask, so I raised my hand. "Yes, Mr. Doyle?" he asked.

"Sir, tell us how you knew his name, his trade, and made the diagnosis so quickly," asked I.

"Elementary observations! His trousers were of the Cameron plaid. The manure on his boot was from cattle, not sheep. The white splatters on his boots and trousers indicated he had been carrying overflowing milk pails. You may have noted that he limped but did not complain of pain. Painless gangrene is typical for diabetes. Any fool should have deduced his weight loss by observing that his belt was buckled three notches down from its usual place. Sadly, there is no cure for Mr. Cameron. An amputation will remove the gangrene and a restricted diet may help for a few months."

The professor waved his hand. "That is all," said he.

After the students left, I greeted Dr. Bell. He shook my hand with a strong grip. "Sir, you are looking well,"

"Lad, what brings you to Auld Reekie?" asked Dr. Bell.

"I intend to qualify for a doctorate in medicine and need your advice," I said.

"You must take an oral examination and write a thesis. Do you have a topic?"

"I am thinking of writing on *tabes dorsalis*. I am quite convinced that the poison of syphilis causes the disease."

"Hmm, not everyone will agree with that notion. I suggest you ask Dr. John Brown for his opinion."

John Brown, one of my other former professors, was the most beloved and wisest physician in all of Scotland. He was also a great writer, which only added to my admiration of him. I immediately called on his office to make an appointment for the next day. Unfortunately, the ancient lady who kept his office said Dr. Brown would be indisposed tomorrow and suggested that I visit his home at 29 Rutland Street the following day.

22 May 1883, Edinburgh

When I arrived at Dr. Brown's home, he greeted me with great cordiality. I presented my proposal for a thesis on *tabes dorsalis*. He was enthusiastic and agreed that the cause was probably syphilis. After we spoke for a wee while, he lay back on a pile of cushions with a great sigh. The color drained from his face. I suspected he had a weak heart but said nothing. He would know his own diagnosis only too well.

"Arthur, will you do a great favor for me?"

"By all means. I would be most happy to do anything for you."

"I am unable to visit a patient. She is Mrs. Samuel Clemens who is residing in the Veitch's family hotel. Would you be so kind as to take a jar of Arnica liniment to her?"

"Yes, indeed," said I.

"Please instruct her to apply the ointment to both knees and then cover them with hot wet towels," he said.

We bid our farewells. Upon my arrival at the home of Mrs. Clemens, a tall man of about fifty years of age, dressed in a white suit and smoking a long cigar, opened the door. He had remarkably unruly, curling, grey hair, a bushy, unkempt mustache, and was surrounded by clouds of tobacco smoke. He extended his hand.

"Mr. Sam Clemens," said he.

Sam Clemens. I knew that name… Could he be THE Samuel Clemens, the writer who had adopted the pen name of Mark Twain? Was this really the great American author here in Edinburgh? I trembled with excitement. His books of adventures were among my favorites, especially after having traveled to the Midwest of America with Dr. Bell nearly five years ago and had seen firsthand the land and people as he had so vividly described. I was amazed, but remembering the reason for my visit, I composed myself.

"Sir, I am Arthur Conan Doyle, here to deliver medicine to Mrs. Clemens."

"Aah, yes. Welcome, Mr. Doyle. I will take you to Mrs. Clemens," he said.

"Sir, by any chance are you Mark Twain, the author of Tom Sawyer?" I asked, just to be sure.

"Guilty as charged," said he.

"I have laughed over whitewashing the fence many times, and I have often dreamed of writing as well as you someday," I said.

"Young man, I would advise you to stick with medicine or find a more useful occupation than writing; drive a steamboat or learn to cheat at cards. Hell and damn, I wrote those stories, but liars and cheats took all my money. I've gone broke a half-dozen times."

"But sir, is the money as important as leaving a mark on the pages of history?" I asked.

Mr. Clemens simply paused, waved away a cloud of smoke, and led me through a large drawing room — part of an extensive suite of rooms — and into an adjoining bedroom. "My wife, Olivia," said he.

Mrs. Clemens was in a large bed, dressed in a nightgown and a shawl, even though it was not yet evening. I observed a half-dozen bottles of medicine on her bedside table, and the curtains were closed.

"Good evening, ma'am. I am Arthur Conan Doyle and have brought you some liniment to ease your pain."

"I was expecting Dr. Brown," said she.

"Dr. Brown is ill."

"Oh, the dear man. I hope it is nothing serious. Young man, are you a physician?"

"Yes, Dr. Brown was one of my professors."

"I suppose you will do. My knees hurt so much. Rheumatism, you know. Please, I am so weak, apply the ointment for me."

She swung her legs over the bed. Though her knees looked to be perfectly normal, I assumed my best bedside manner, sat on a chair, and carefully massaged a generous dab of the ointment into the little depressions beside her kneecaps. "Oh, that feels so good," she said when I applied towels, which had been soaked in hot water and wrung out. "I am so much better. You are a kind young man. Will you visit tomorrow?" she asked.

I bowed. "If Dr. Brown is unable to make a call, I will be happy to see you again."

I was making my way out of the suite when Mr. Clemens plucked at my elbow. "Livy has been in such pain . . . We are grateful for your service. Say, I am lecturing at the Queen's theatre tomorrow evening, and after my lecture, the Siamese twins, Sui Fong and Wei Fong, will sing and dance. Kindly accept these two tickets. Who knows? It may inspire you to seize upon an idea for your first novel." He winked and showed me to the door.

"Thank you, sir. It would be an honor," I said, before taking the tickets and making my exit.

24 May 1883, Edinburgh

I carry my notebook with me as often as possible in order to capture and recall moments such as I have experienced in the last few hours.

It began when I invited Miss Jean McGill, a student at the university, to accompany me to the performance. Jean is a little on the plump side, but I had been in love with her for almost two weeks a couple of years ago while I was finishing medical school and right before I left for Russia with Dr. Bell. She reluctantly agreed to join me only after I explained that Siamese twins were a medical curiosity. Jean desperately wanted to be a doctor, but the faculty of medicine would not allow her to dissect in the anatomy laboratory.

Thanks to Mr. Clemens, our seats were front row, center. The Queen's Theatre was packed to the top gallery with spectators anxious to hear the great American author's speak, see the famous Siamese twins and listen to them sing. Gas lights lit the stage as bright as day, but the far recesses were in shadows.

When the curtain went up, a young man came out and announced the arrival of 'Mr. Mark Twain' who sauntered in from the left wing, sat on a high stool, and winked at the audience. He puffed at his ever-present stogie, removed it from his mouth, and peered at the ash on the end. "I never can get rid of the damn ash," he said.

He squinted at the audience, shrugged his shoulders and, after another moment of silence, went off on a mile-a-minute monologue.

"This morning, when the sun was bright and shining, a Scotch banker loaned me his umbrella. It was mighty kind of him although there was no rain in sight. I supposed he was kind and generous. Well, by and by, clouds came in and water poured out of the heavens. I would have been drenched had it not been for the kindness of the banker, but in the midst of the downpour, he not only demanded I return the umbrella but insisted I pay a dollar interest for its use." The crowd clapped tepidly, mostly out of politeness. There wasn't much enthusiasm for jokes at the expense of Scotsmen, not even if the butt of the joke was a banker.

Mr. Twain puffed his cigar, took a long look at the lengthening ash, and launched into a story about a frog named Dan'l Webster that "could jump further than any other frog in the entire state of Californy." The owner of the frog took bets on how far the frog could jump, but someone loaded Dan'l Webster with birdshot and he couldn't jump even one inch. When the laughing and feet stomping stopped, Mr. Twain told another whopper, this time about a duel between two newspaper editors in Nevada who lit out at each other with Colt six-shooters. They were bad shots, and no one was seriously hurt. He left the stage with a flourish. The cigar was down to about one and one-half inches, but the ash had never fallen off. I suspect he had a pin down the middle of his stogie.

Miss McGill never cracked a smile. She didn't care for Yankee humor, and when I was romantically inclined, she pushed away my hand. She perked up when a small, black-haired Italian man, Signor Bellini, introduced the Siamese twins, Wei and Sui. According to the program, the twins were trained in the Italian school of bel canto singing. Signor Bellini claimed the twins were favorites of the Chinese emperor and had performed before the heads of state of every country from China to Scotland. They swept onto the stage, dressed in a white, gossamer gown that floated in the air and enveloped both of them as if they had the wings of butterflies. Wei and Sui were beautiful, with an exotic Eurasian cast to their features. Their eyes were as dark as bits of obsidian, and their long, coal-black hair appeared to have been varnished. There was, however, a distinct English cast to their features. They bowed in unison. Then, Sui Fong — on the right — played a long, stringed instrument that made a noise like a wailing screech owl, and both twins sang trills and long runs of high notes with turns and leaps of sound. Jean was spellbound and clapped with great emotion at the end of each song. I was relieved to see how much she enjoyed that portion of the evening's entertainment.

After the last encore, the stage lights dimmed while the crowd cheered and clapped. On stage, a tallish man, dressed in a formal evening suit and wearing a top hat with the brim pulled down over his face, emerged from the shadows. He carried a cloth-covered tray with two flutes of what appeared to be champagne. It seemed to be a part of the final act. For a fleeting moment, I was certain that Wei Fong smiled in recognition of the man. She took a glass and downed the champagne in a single gulp. Sui Fong took the second glass, hesitated, and took a delicate sip. The fellow dashed from the stage and disappeared into the shadows, but as soon as the crowd hurrahed at this presumed encore, Wei dropped her empty glass, grasped her throat, and collapsed onto the stage, dragging down her sister. Sui's barely-touched glass fell and shattered, splashing the stage with champagne. The crowd was stunned into silence, which was followed by a great, collective gasp. At first, individuals, then entire rows of people, dashed to the exits as if someone had shouted "Fire!" The Italian agent, Bellini, came out of the wings and, with an anguished cry, wiped Wei's face with a frilly handkerchief. She had evidently suffered some form of an attack and needed medical attention. I leaped onto the stage and knelt by the stricken woman. In a moment, her face took on a blue tinge and she went perfectly limp. I felt for her pulse at the wrist. Nothing! Then, I dug my fingers into her neck. The beat of the carotid artery was too rapid to count, became fluttery, hesitated, and then resumed its frantic, erratic pace. Sui rolled and twisted on the stage as if attempting to separate herself from Wei. "Is she going to die?" she asked.

"I, I don't know," said I.

"If my sister dies, I shall die with her. Oh, it was so bitter."

I crouched by the sisters, with my finger on Wei's fluttery pulse. "Arthur, you are a doctor! Do something!" Jean McGill shouted in my ear.

"We shall both die. Oh, it was so bitter ..." Sui whimpered.

Bitter, bitter, what would be bitter? I thought. *Some sort of a poison, but what?* It came to me in a flash; Wei had the symptoms of an overdose of Gelsemium; she was weak in her extremities, her respiratory muscles were paralyzed, and she had rapid, irregular heartbeats.

16

"Send immediately for Dr. Bell!" I shouted. I then pressed down on Wei's chest to drive out the old air and pulled her arms over her head to force fresh air into her lungs. It was a technique called 'artificial respiration,' and I had seen it used on patients who had been overdosed with chloroform. I pressed her chest and raised her arms again and again with a ferocious sense that I must save her life. Color returned to her cheeks for a few minutes, but I was unable to force enough oxygen into her body. Sui moaned and she, too, appeared to be on the verge of collapse. Had she taken a fatal dose of the poison? I should have pumped out her stomach, but had no tube. At that moment, Mark Twain rushed onto the stage, still chewing his cigar. I snatched it out of his mouth and jammed the saliva soaked wad of tobacco into Sui's mouth. She gagged, choked, coughed, and vomited up the contents of her stomach. This had taken just a moment, but by the time I turned my attention back to Wei and resumed pressing on her chest, she had already faded away. Her heart stopped. I knelt by her side, overcome by a sense of utter helplessness. Sui gave a great sigh. To my utter horror, she had become pale. Her eyes rolled up, and the color had drained from her cheeks. Drained . . . Drained? God, I was such a fool. Wei was dead, but the twins were connected so that Sui's heart pumped blood into Wei's circulation. That was what Sui meant when she said they would both die. I tore away the gossamer dress and found a band of tissue as big around as my arm connecting the twins at their waist.

"Great Scott! She is bleeding into her dead sister. Ye damn fool — a tourniquet, use your belt man!" I heard Dr. Bell shout. He had arrived with Willum, his man, who carried an instrument case. I removed my belt, wrapped it around the band of tissue and cinched it down as tight as possible. Sui was still alive, but just barely. Dr. Bell kneeled on the stage and stroked Sui's hair. "I will not let you die," he said. A bit of color returned to Sui's cheeks, but she breathed rapidly and I could barely feel her pulse. "There isn't a moment to lose. We must remove her to a place suitable for surgery," said Dr. Bell.

"But, sir, in the history of surgery, no one — absolutely no one — has separated Siamese twins," said I.

"We are duty-bound to save her life if we can and must make the attempt," Dr. Bell replied.

Mark Twain listened to our conversation, lit another cigar, and looked down at the poor twins. "I have a spare room in my hotel across the street," he said.

Willing hands carried the live girl, attached to her dead sister, through the theatre, out the lobby, and across the street to the hotel. It was a grim procession made even gloomier by drizzly rain and the curtain of yellow fog that enveloped Edinburgh. It occurred to me halfway across the street that the killer could be lurking about. "Jean, I can call a cab to take you home," said I.

"You can't get rid of me that easily. I shall stay and help," she snapped.

Dr. Bell decided on the dining room in the Twain apartment, where there were bright, gas lights. We placed the twins on a wide, mahogany table and rapidly soaked the instruments in a basin of water and carbolic acid. We rolled up our sleeves and rinsed our hands. Despite the urgency, Dr. Bell strictly adhered to the antiseptic technique. A bit of color had returned to Sui's cheeks. It was a good sign, but she opened her eyes like a startled fawn and looked in horror at the array of steel knives, forceps, needles and thread on the table.

"Miss McGill, give the chloroform," said Dr. Bell.

"I have never given an anaesthetic," Jean said.

"Pour the chloroform, a few drops at a time, on a folded cloth held over her face until she goes to sleep. If her breathing slows, stop pouring. If she moves, give more," said Dr. Bell.

Sui struggled at the first whiff of chloroform, but soon settled into a light sleep. Jean gained confidence and was able to adjust the dose of chloroform so our patient remained unconscious. Dr. Bell, with sleeves rolled to his elbows and his sharpest scalpel in hand, surveyed the band of flesh that connected the abdomens of the live and dead twins.

"Arthur, move the tourniquet closer to Sui, if you please," said Dr. Bell. I adjusted the belt. The incision was perfectly bloodless, since no blood circulated on Wei's side and my tourniquet cut off the blood flow from Sui. He pressed the knife deeper into the tissue until a layer that looked like the lining of the abdominal cavity came into view. There was indeed a cavity, and within the space, there was a solid, brownish-colored organ. "Aha, they shared a common liver," said Dr. Bell.

"It is hopeless," said I.

"Perhaps, but we shall see." He cut into the liver and exposed a nest of blood vessels which he sutured with a silk thread.

"Now, release the tourniquet." I loosened the belt. A gush of blood literally exploded from the cut surface of the liver.

"I can barely feel her pulse," said Jean.

"Tighten the tourniquet and stop giving chloroform," said Dr. Bell. He sutured more blood vessels, but each time I released the tourniquet, there was a gush of blood.

"Damn me. An old fashioned hot iron would sear these vessels," said Dr. Bell.

"Sir, I will heat an amputation knife in the flame of a gas light," I replied.

It seemed to take hours, though it was only a few minutes until the blade glowed red hot in the gas flame. Dr. Bell held the wooden handle and pressed the blade against the surface of the liver. There was smoke and a *sizzle* as the blade burned the tissue. I released the tourniquet again. This time, there was only a slow ooze of blood from the cut surface. With two more slashes, Dr. Bell divided the liver with the red-hot knife. There was only a little bleeding, which he controlled with sutures. He incised through the remaining skin until he had separated the dead from the living. Bell sutured the skin so that only a neat row of stitches showed where Sui had once been connected to her twin.

"The pulse is stronger," Jean said.

Angry voices came from the next room, and in a moment, Detective McPherson and a constable from the Edinburgh Police burst into the room. McPherson was a big-shouldered bully who had played rugby on the town teams against us students. He took in the blood-soaked table, the instruments, and the dead girl at a glance. "A murder was reported, but this is more than murder. What foul deeds are you up to?"

"We saved a life. Yes, there was a murder — a foul murder — but in the theatre, not here," said Dr. Bell.

"Yes, murder by poison, namely an overdose of Gelsemium," said I.

"The doctors are correct. I witnessed the death of the twin, Wei. The other would have died as well, without these medical gentlemen," said Mr. Twain.

McPherson's face grew red with frustration and anger. Having the chance to arrest a professor and an old school boy would enhance his reputation. "This is no regular hospital. How do I know she did not die under your knife from a dastardly experiment?"

Sui fluttered her eyes and came awake with a low moan. Miss McGill stroked her face and spoke softly. "I saw the whole thing." She told the story from beginning to end, effectively ending the detective's tirade. I could have kissed her.

"An autopsy on Wei will prove everything," said Dr. Bell.

Willum carried Sui to the spare room while the constables wrapped Wei's corpse in a blanket and carried her away to the morgue. Dr. Bell packed up his instruments and ordered me to stand vigil over Sui. I commenced my bedside duties and, in my focus on keeping watch, I forgot about Miss McGill, who must have found her own way home.

I had no nursing skills, could not even make up a bed, but kept my fingers on her pulse, offered sips of water when she stirred, and said soothing words. Fortunately, the girl slept most of the time while I was on bedside watch. Promptly at six a.m., a Nightingale nurse, dressed in a pure white uniform with an apron that reached her ankles, bustled into the room. "A gude mornin' to ye, Meester Doyle. Dr. Bell directed me to care for the poor lass. Miss Angeline McTavish at your service," she said. Miss McTavish was a plain lady, approaching middle age, and wonderfully efficient. She fluffed the pillows, changed the sheet, wiped Sui's face with a wet cloth, and swabbed her lips with glycerin. The girl came awake with a startled cry and wild, frightened eyes.

"Oh, where is my sister? Where is Wei?" She flung herself about the bed until I worried about the stitches. "I am all alone!" sobbed Sui.

I took her hand, gave it a reassuring squeeze, and floundered as I grasped for the right words. "There was an accident. You are fine, but Wei is dead." This was not the first time I had told a poor, grieving soul about their relative's death, but this was different. After all, a part of Sui had died, as well, since they had been together every minute of their lives.

My words were totally inadequate, but Miss McTavish came to my rescue. "There, there, dear. Time for some wee rest. Ye'll be needin' all o' yer strength to get back upon your toes, y'know. I will be here wi' ye today so yer nae alone. Mr. Doyle, dinna' forget you are to meet the good doctor in the morgue promptly at eight this very mornin'. He will surely be upset if you are late. Rest assured, I will stay here with Miss Fong and take good care o' the lass," said she.

After thanking Miss McTavish for her assistance, I brushed out the wrinkles in my suit and took a cup of tea in the hotel lobby before rushing away to the infirmary. I was a few minutes late. The old morgue in the basement of the Royal Infirmary was cold, dark, and as depressing as ever. To my surprise, three of Edinburgh's leading surgeons had gathered to witness the dissection and see Dr. Bell's handiwork. With clouds of tobacco smoke, Spence, Arbuthnot, and Archer masked the odors of rotting flesh, intestinal gas, and the general putrefaction that permeated the very walls.

Two gas lights were focused on the dissecting table but the rest of the room was in shadows. I noted the presence of McPherson and his two constables hovering in the background and then, to my amazement, recognized Sherlock Holmes. He must have arrived on the night express from London, but impeccably turned out in a pearl grey cutaway morning coat, a winged collar and a perfectly tied cravat. He barely nodded in my direction and I made no comment.

The surgeons intently examined the liver in the band of flesh that had connected the twins.

"Confoundedly impossible. Bell, old boy, how did you stop the hemorrhage?" asked Spence. Before Dr. Bell could answer, Professor Lewis made the long, Y-shaped incision typical of an autopsy, which commenced at Wei's upper chest and extended down her abdomen. One by one, Professor Lewis examined and

21

removed each organ until the heart, lungs, liver, spleen, and intestinal tract lay on a steel dish. Detective McPherson groaned with disappointment as Professor Lewis pronounced each organ normal. "I understand there is a suspicion of death by poison," said Professor Lewis.

At that moment, Sherlock Holmes stepped out of the shadows. "May I open the Stomach?"

"No, highly irregular," Professor Lewis said.

"Mr. Holmes is a trained anatomist and, I believe is now with Her Majesties Secret Service," Dr. Bell said.

The professor made a slight bow, "In that case, by all means, Mr. Holmes may have the honor."

Holmes withdrew a small instrument case from an inner coat pocket, selected a pointed bistoury, a scoop and two curved retractors with sharp points. He inserted a retractor in the wall of the stomach. "Mr. Doyle, if you please?"

I held the one retractor while he inserted the second and held the stomach so the contents would not spill. Homes then opened the stomach with the bistoury, sniffed the contents, and scooped out an ounce of fluid, which he spread on the steel dish.

For at least ten minutes, he minutely examined the stomach's contents with a hand lens. At last, satisfied, he passed the lens to Professor Lewis. "There are bits of undigested food, nothing else," the professor said.

"Observe, if you will the tiny golden globules. They, undoubtedly are the golden starlet caviar, usually reserved for the Russian Royal Family," Holmes said. Dr. Bell, Professor Lewis and the assembled doctors, in turn examined the material. "Yes, I do believe you are correct," Professor Lewis exclaimed. "But what is the meaning of this?"

Holmes did not answer, but remarked, "In addition, by the odor, there are traces of the drug, Gelsemium, in the specimen."

"Gelemium is hardly a poison," Professor Lewis exclaimed.

"Mr. Doyle, tell us how the death occurred," Holmes said.

I repeated my story about the strange man who had appeared from the shadows and given the twins the fatal draught. "Mr.

Holmes is correct, Wei died with all the symptoms of an overdose of Gelsemium," I said.

"What makes you an authority of Gelsemium?" asked McPherson.

"I published a paper on the toxic effects of the drug in the *British Medical and Surgical Journal*," I said.

"It was a well done paper," said Dr. Bell.

Professor Lewis sniffed at the yellow liquid from Wei's stomach as if it were a fine wine. "Ah, I will wager the young man is correct. I shall analyze the contents later today. Now, laddie, tell these gentlemen about Gelsemium," said the professor.

"It is an extract of the roots of Yellow Jasmine, a flowering plant found in the southern part of the United States of America. It is used in appropriate doses to treat nerve pain and muscle spasm."

"Arthur, you made an astute diagnosis. Well done, lad. I am proud of you," said Holmes.

"And I second that," Dr. Bell said.

"Thank you, sir."

"Mr. Holmes, Arthur, will you kindly join me for dinner at my home this evening? Would eight o'clock be convenient?" He asked.

"Yes, of course, but I don't have an evening suit with me," I answered.

"Quite alright, my boy. We shall be informal."

I immediately returned to Sui's bedside. To my amazement, she was sitting with her back against fluffy pillows, taking strong, beef broth. When she finished, Miss McTavish gave her a spoonful of tincture of iron. Sui spluttered, and although she appeared wan, her face was wreathed in a smile that melted my heart. In a moment, she took my hand in hers. "Mr. Twain told me everything. You saved my life," said Sui.

"Ah noo, but I am leaving you in good hands," said the nurse. She threw on her cloak and swished out the door, leaving me alone with Sui.

"I must thank you. May I give you a kiss for saving me?" Sui put her arms around my neck, lowered her eye lashes, kissed my cheek, and let her soft lips linger as they brushed across my skin.

It would be unethical to kiss a patient, but oh how I wished to turn my face and feel the smoothness of her lips on mine. As she leaned towards me, Sui's nightdress dropped ever so slightly, revealing perfect shoulders and a hint of bosom. I caught my breath, wishing the situation were different and I could act on my desire and meet her open lips. It was difficult not to get caught up in the blissfulness of the moment, especially when she made a slight groan, but I managed to retain my professional composure and quickly pulled back.

"Dear Sui, I am forgetting myself. Did I hurt your incision?"

"Now that you have saved me and we are better acquainted, you may call me Julie. My real name is Julie Pembroke. My sister's name was Mildred. Sui and Wei were only our stage names." She spoke in perfect, rapid English, as if she urgently needed to tell her story. My head swam. I was confused. Who was this delightful woman? Was she Chinese or English?

"I don't understand. Why did you perform under different names?"

"When Papa died — was killed, actually — in the Afghanistan war, Uncle Peachy became our guardian and arranged for our education in languages and music. We already spoke Chinese and English, but he said we must make our own way in life, and being Siamese twins, that meant performing on the stage or joining a freak show. Uncle Peachy had other ideas as well. We actually did a bit of work for Uncle."

"What kind of work?" I asked.

Julie blushed and turned away. "Oh, at first it was just for fun. We, especially Mildred, attracted men, and a certain sort wanted both of us. They talked, and sometimes, we learned secrets for Uncle Peachy."

I wanted to reach out to her and offer the comfort of my firm embrace. Instead, I held back, especially since, at that moment, Julie's face twisted with fierce intensity as if she were remembering something painful. "Did you see him? Could you recognize the man who killed my sister?" she asked, after a long silence.

"It was very dark. I had only a glimpse, and his face was hidden. I thought for a moment that Wei, er, Mildred recognized him," said I.

"It must have been one of them, one of her visitors. Uncle Peachy warned us to be careful. I thought he had a scent, something with spice," said Julie.

At that moment, another Nightingale nurse bustled into the room carrying a covered tray. I bid the ladies good evening and went home to Mam for a bit of rest before dinner with Dr. Bell.

I arrived at Dr. Bell's promptly at eight o'clock. Willum met me at the door, took my umbrella, and led me into the study. Holmes was seated in a deep leather chair with his legs extended and his long fine hands folded on his lap. He barely nodded at my entrance.

I immediately recognized Colonel Sir Cameron Beachy-Edwards who I had met when my Uncle Declan was murdered years ago. He also came to Russia when Dr. Bell and I traveled there in 1881 and helped us save the Crown from a potential war. Now, he sat opposite Dr. Bell by a grate with glowing coals. A bottle of Old Glenmore sat on the table between them. With the help of his walking stick, Colonel Beachy-Edwards rose to his feet with some difficulty and extended his hand. "Arthur, dear boy, how can I express my deepest gratitude? Your quick thinking saved Julie Pembroke," said he.

As usual, in the presence of the regal Colonel, I came to attention and, as if still a poor, young student, felt shabby in my threadbare tweeds. He was impeccably dressed in striped trousers, a black, frock coat, and the ever-present Victoria Cross ribbon over his breast; his clothing was looser than I remembered from our Russian adventure. He had lost weight and appeared ill.

"I am sorry that I could not have done more," I said.

A tear glistened in his eye. "You did your best. I am responsible for the twins, but sadly, I now realize I put them in too great a danger. You see, the twins are my wards."

"You are 'Uncle Peachy'?" I asked. The colonel blushed to the roots of his hair.

"Yes, the twins called me Uncle Peachy from the day I became their guardian. Their father was an officer in my regiment. He married a Portuguese-Chinese woman. It was a dreadful scandal, but she was beautiful and kind and ultimately won the hearts of every officer." The colonel paused and wiped a tear that trickled down his cheek.

"She was quite small and died in childbirth. Captain Pembroke, fearful of ridicule, kept the twins in seclusion but provided them with a superior education. I was their godfather. When he died of wounds in Afghanistan, I became their guardian and, later, brought them to England. There was very little money in the captain's estate, so they had to make their way in the world. I arranged for music lessons, and they became fluent in Mandarin, Russian, and French, as well as English. Men with strange appetites were drawn to them, but the twins were skilled in fending them off. As they got older, however, they insisted I give them assignments in service of the Crown. It was their way of repaying what they thought of as a debt. Because of their unique circumstances, they gained secret information that some men spilled in moments of passion. They insisted on performing these covert activities against my will. They were headstrong, and I have had no experience controlling young ladies. Mildred was especially skilled and could easily have become a courtesan except for her highly developed sense of right and wrong. One of those men could have been the murderer, especially if he was afraid he had 'spilled some beans' as they say."

"Sir, they were inseparable. I don't understand how Wei, er, Mildred, could have had a private tête-à-tête without the knowledge of Julie. I should also think that a man would be embarrassed," I said.

When Sir Cameron Beachy-Edwards assumed his role as a professor, I felt inadequate — and even stupid — because he seemed to think that I should be aware of the most obscure information. "Arthur, surely you must know that a Siamese twin has the ability to go into a trance-like state and be completely oblivious to the activities of her sibling. In fact, Mr. Samuel Clemens, under his nom de plume, Mark Twain, remarked on this in his essay of

Chang and Eng, each of whom were married and had children. I can assure you, Julie had no knowledge of the men whom Mildred entertained," said the colonel.

During this entire conversation, or should I say, a lecture, Sherlock Holmes had said nothing. His eyes were half closed, but I sensed his acute perception of the Colonels words. He now sprung to his feet and paced the floor to the fireplace, then returned to face the Colonel.

"Sir, the murder, for that is the word has the earmarks of a Russian, a most accomplished, evil Russian,"

Colonel, Sir Beach-Edwards nodded, "you are quite right."

"How, how can you make that assumption?" I asked.

"Simple, the presence of caviar in the victim's stomach. Now, I must hasten back to London. If you will excuse me," Holmes replied.

We bid farewell to the enigmatic Holmes and retired, once again, to the drawing room.

"Arthur, would you like a drop of a fine single malt?" asked Dr. Bell, as if to offer me a reprieve from my confusion.

"Indeed, sir."

Willum brought up a chair, and I joined the group around the table. The smooth whisky slid down my throat, and I sunk into the comfort of a deep cushion and the warmth of companionship. My days in practice at Southsea had been lonely.

Dr. Bell took a sip of Old Glenmore, put down his glass, and folded his hands across his chest. "Arthur, we have traveled over oceans to America and Russia together and you have proven yourself to be a fine companion, doctor, and even life-saving sleuth. Are you up for another adventure? Dr. Reginald Fitz at Harvard has invited me to Boston for a series of lectures and demonstrations. It seems as if the Americans still don't believe in Lister's work with antisepsis. Professor Fitz has not yet convinced the Americans to operate for appendicitis. We will then go on to San Francisco where I am to lecture on surgery in children with tuberculosis at the American Society of Surgery."

I considered the prospect of traveling to America again and exploring even farther west than we'd gone back in 1878. We certainly had our share of discoveries and daring adventures, and the remembrance of surviving many mishaps together — on land, at sea, and even aloft — made me smile.

Returning from my nostalgic daydream, I realized it would be difficult to leave my patients for more than just a few days and could even diminish my practice further. "I would like to go but cannot leave my practice in Southsea," said I.

The colonel tapped his cane. "I insist you accompany Dr. Bell," said he.

"I am afraid that would be impossible right now, sir. My patients depend on my services."

"You swore allegiance to the Queen and are still under oath to serve the Crown," said the colonel.

"Yes, sir, but my practice is my only livelihood and I must help support my mam and family," said I.

"You see no more than two or three patients a day, is that right?" asked the colonel.

I hung my head in shame. How could he know that I was a failure, that the practice did not yet even support the rent? If I left my few patients, even if only for a short while, they would quickly find another doctor and I would lose everything.

The colonel's voice grew cold. "If you don't agree, the Crown will revoke your medical license. There is no need to worry about your practice. I have a friend, an army surgeon who has recently retired, who is now taking a refresher course at St. Bartholomew's Hospital. His name is John Watson, and he would be happy to take over your practice for two months."

I had known a John Watson at university. He was a good man. I was angry at the colonel for cornering me this way. Why would he put me in this position? Had I not done enough for the Crown when Dr. Bell and I last traveled to Russia and helped prevent an international conflict? The colonel, as head of the Secret Service, held the power of the British Empire in his hands. The damn empire had done nothing for us Scots and Irish, but I knew better than to argue, so I just held my tongue and glowered with suppressed rage.

"Doyle, my boy, the game is afoot yet again. I assure you this will be an opportunity for you to advance professionally, and you will be well paid," said Dr. Bell.

Something in me softened at hearing Dr. Bell's words. I did enjoy the adventures with him and seeing the world. "What duties must I perform, if I go?" asked I.

The good doctor rose and rummaged through the smoking paraphernalia that littered the mantle. From the heap of pouches, straight-stemmed churchwarden pipes, and lovely old meerschaums, he selected an enormous calabash that he deliberately filled with Cavendish. When he had tamped down the tobacco and lit the pipe with a coal from the grate, he exhaled a cloud of smoke. "Ah, the gourd stem ensures a cool smoke. Now, Arthur, you will assist me during surgery and arrange patients for demonstration. As with our other trips, there may also be some risk involved, so we need to be vigilant. The colonel will explain your ancillary duties," said Bell.

Ancillary duties? It was clear they had already discussed the matter and decided that I would accompany them. I could not say no to Dr. Bell. By assisting him on this journey I would learn more medicine that would be valuable in my practice. The additional compensation would certainly help pay rent, and then some. However, I was wary about what else might be required and what they meant by 'ancillary duties' . . .

The colonel again rose stiffly and went to a large globe of the world. "Here is the North Pacific, rimmed by the United States, Russia, China, Japan, the Philippines, and ..." He paused to tap the globe for emphasis. "The damn Yankees control the Sandwich Islands and have what was formerly Russian-America. They have recently acquired a coaling station in Korea, are making inroads into Japan, and are contemplating a canal through Central America. The Americans have never forgiven us for supplying the Confederate States during their Civil War and are still demanding reparations for the battle cruiser, *Shenandoah*, which we outfitted for the South. The Americans are determined to have total control over the Pacific Ocean. Our only port on the North Pacific is British Columbia."

"This is all very interesting, but doesn't involve me. I did enough for the Crown in Russia and nearly died in the process — with no thanks, I might add. Mr. Holmes is far better equipped for this work," I said.

The colonel ignored me and went on, as if I was a mere insect. "The Russians claim that the land they sold to the Americans also included the entire west coast down to the Oregon Territory. Now, the Americans want that as well. The Queen appreciated your work, but, as you well know, the affair with the Tsar is so sensitive the international repercussions would be disastrous for England. Your work must never be made public. You are still under oath to the Crown. As for Mr. Holmes, I have other tasks for him."

"Sir, I think I have had enough of our fanciful and risky trips and desire only to get on with my practice of medicine and write a novel," I said.

The colonel took a generous measure of the single malt and forced a wan smile. "Would you not value the opportunity to solidify your finances, learn about the latest medical trends, and show your loyalty to the Crown while also working to track down the man who murdered Mildred? Poor Julie might recognize the man and be in danger. Duty demands that I send her to America, since the killer might well be in a plot against England."

What an enticing prospect. Momentarily drunk with the fantasy of finding Mildred's killer and having Julie show her gratitude with her soft lips on mine, I almost agreed on the spot, until I reminded myself that I cannot afford to become seriously involved with a woman until my practice is flourishing, to say nothing of the fact that she is still my patient.

"Instead of Sherlock Holmes, Lady Penelope Walshingham will accompany Miss Pembroke to America as her traveling companion," continued the colonel. Was that a smile or smirk on his face as he made this announcement?

I gasped at the thought of seeing Penelope again; blood rushed to my face. I had been madly in love — was it love — with the ever-mysterious, tantalizing Penelope during our Russian adventure, despite believing her to be a double — or was it a triple — agent. She worked for the Crown, but may have also been a

30

German spy, the mistress of the Prince of Wales, and who knows what else . . .

"Sir, Miss Walshingham is a treacherous double agent and should have been executed for treason. How can you trust her?" I asked. I was intrigued by prospect of seeing her again and admittedly had often thought of Penelope and our many stolen kisses.

"Penelope expected to marry the prince and be the next queen, but he would not divorce his wife. Penelope threatened to expose the prince for the gambling, womanizing playboy that he is. The Crown was happy to buy her off by dropping charges and re-instating her in the Secret Service."

"Gentlemen, it is time for dinner. Let us continue this discussion later," said Dr. Bell.

The food was good, plain Scottish fare; barley soup, mutton, boiled potatoes, and haggis. I had second helpings of everything. After the rice pudding, we filed back to the study where Willum had laid out a bottle of Madeira and a round of cheese.

"Look at it this way, Arthur. Julie is in great danger. You could be of service to her," said the colonel. "And to Miss Walshingham, as well..." he added.

He had touched my weak spot and he knew it. I love nothing more than old tales of chivalry and derring-do, especially when they involve a beautiful woman. Dr. Bell knows me well. He had been wise to take a break in the conversation after the talk of going with Julie to America and the first mention of Penelope. He must have figured that pondering the idea of another international quest while being sated by indulging in a delicious meal was the best way to gain my acquiescence. It worked. "I have given it some thought and agree to accompany Dr. Bell," I said.

"You are a wise and brave lad. You will go with Dr. Bell to America and render what assistance you can to Miss Pembroke. I will arrange for Dr. Watson to cover your practice while you are abroad. We will let your patients know you are temporarily away in pursuit of new techniques so they can be assured they will get the best, and most current, care on your return."

31

With the decision made, and more briskness than he had exhibited so far in the evening, Colonel Beachy-Edwards opened a large carton and brought out a black walking stick with a peculiar handle. "This may be useful." He twisted the handle to reveal a revolving cylinder. "The outer layer of ebony covers a .32 calibre rifled barrel. It is capable of firing three shots. You simply twist the cylinder and press the concealed trigger. When the muzzle is pressed against a vital spot, one shot will kill instantly, and it is accurate up to a distance of some thirty feet."

He next produced a lovely, leather gentleman's traveling case, which contained a razor, soap, spare buttons, needle and thread, a small nail file, and a silver liquor flask. "By pressing this button, you can open a secret compartment, which contains spare bullets for the cane and a small stiletto. You have everything necessary for self-defense, and this." The colonel rather gingerly picked out the silver liquor flask. "Be extremely careful. This flask contains black powder. Twisting the lid ignites a spark and a ten-second fuse that, in turn, sets off an explosion with sufficient smoke and noise to confuse your enemies."

"Will we be in constant danger?" I asked.

"You must be willing to take risks because the empire may be at stake. I would go with you, but duty calls in London. You and Dr. Bell have the particular skill of making keen observations, which, in your previous travels, has proven to be advantageous. Once again, you will need to be aware and use your wits to stay out of trouble," the colonel said.

"Arthur, I am indeed pleased with your decision. I am sure we can learn something new from the Americans. Professor Fitz will teach us about this new disease, appendicitis," said Dr. Bell.

"Gentlemen, I must take my leave." The colonel rose, rather stiffly. Willum immediately appeared with his hat and cloak.

Dr. Bell was as excited as a schoolboy when he pushed aside the bottle and unrolled a map of North America on the table. "We leave from Liverpool on the *Oregon*, a new Cunard Liner, on the thirtieth of May and will arrive in Boston seven days later. She is the fastest ship afloat. We shall spend nearly a week in Boston and then onto Chicago. Our good friend the railroad baron, Angus

Duncan has arranged first-class accommodations all the way to San Francisco."

Perhaps it was the meal and wine, but I had already warmed to the idea of another adventure and traveling again with Dr. Bell. My practice had been dull and unsuccessful thus far, to say the least, and as with our previous experiences in America and Russia, I would commit to keeping a diary of each experience in order to have an official record and amass more material for my novel.

"We shall see the Rocky Mountains and perhaps a herd of buffalo," I said. "I have read that the Indians are still ferocious and there are bandits in the west."

"The American Army has the Indians under control. Besides, I have my sword cane and a Webley .455. Thanks to the colonel, you are also well armed. We have more than enough firepower to subdue aboriginals and ruffians," said Dr. Bell.

It was nearly time to leave. "Now Arthur, we will be in a first-class salon on the ship and you must look the part of a respectable physician. Since at least one of the suits you had made for our journey to Russia was destroyed by that swordsman, I suggest you acquire some new clothing, as you have done with our last two trips."

25 May 1883

I had only enough time to be measured for a lightweight summer outfit and a new evening suit at the local haberdashery today before racing back to Southsea to meet Dr. Watson and gather personal belongings for the journey. Dr. Watson appeared to be a perfectly competent physician. I am happy to leave my practice in his able hands. Unfortunately, there was no time for us to become better acquainted, but I trust the colonel's judgement. Truth be told, I will get some time away from a practice which reminds me I have not yet achieved success, and if Bell is right, I will return better able to serve my patients and build my practice.

27 May 1883, Edinburgh

This morning, I went directly from the train station to the bedside of Miss Pembroke. Mr. Twain greeted me with a wave of his cigar. I have never met such a friendly man. Oh, that all Americans were so delightful. Julie had made an amazing recovery. She was up, and I couldn't help but notice that she was dressed in an adorable gown that showed her trim body to the best advantage while concealing the site where she had been connected to her sister.

"I am here to inspect your incision," said I.

"There is no need. Dr. Bell changed the dressings this morning." I had hoped for at least a friendly smile, but she was distant. I attributed her demeanor to a post-operative, depressed mental state. I thought surely, despite her great loss, when she learned that I was to be her guardian on the journey, she would be delighted and even melt in my arms, knowing I would take care of her. Instead, she simply brushed aside a stray lock of hair and sipped from a cup of tea.

"Uncle Peachy said you will be traveling on the *Oregon*," said she.

"Aye. Perhaps we will meet on the ship," I said.

Julie simply tossed her head and made no response. I should have been more sensitive to her great loss. After all, her twin was really a part of her.

30 May 1883

Last night, I collected my new outfits from the haberdashers, packed everything in my portmanteau, kissed Mam goodbye, and arrived at the station a little after midnight in time to board the train with Dr. Bell. The trip to Liverpool was uneventful. We hired a cab drawn by a pair of fast, chestnut mares for the mad dash from the rail station to the docks. I was excited by the prospect of our upcoming travels and had come around to feeling completely at ease with taking leave from my humdrum medical practice. The bustling Port of Liverpool was crammed with towers, cranes, and machines of all sizes and description for the handling of cargo. The yellow waters of the Mersey were busier than ever with steamships carrying immigrants to the new world. Tug boats chugged back and forth while stevedores, all hooting and shouting, unloaded cargo amidst a tangle of horses and wagons. Our cab drew up next to the *Oregon* amidst carriages and broughams, which had carried the hundreds of impatient passengers now attempting to board the ship at the same time.

The *Oregon*, moored to the Prince's Dock at the foot of Bath Street, was over five hundred feet in length and powered by enormous steam engines. She also carried four masts to catch a following wind. *Soon,* I thought, *even these auxiliary sails will be obsolete.* The Union Jack and the Cunard pennant fluttered at her stern.

We boarded at the first-class gangway with the rich and famous, all excited to be aboard for the fastest crossing of the Atlantic ever made. Back aft, the poor, the lonely, and the unwanted struggled up the gangway, escaping old Europe for a better life in the New World. Sailors wearing smart uniforms lined her deck, while Captain Cottier welcomed us first-class passengers. There was great excitement because the *Oregon* had made the crossing from Boston in seven days. The captain promised the return voyage would take only six and one-half days. The Royal Marine Band, with trumpets flashing in the sun, played a rousing version of "Rule Britannia." Stevedores took Dr. Bell's bags and trunk, and my lone portmanteau, but the professor insisted that I carry his precious instrument case. I was at his side, feeling hot and a bit shabby in my old, tweed, traveling jacket, when Julie and Penelope swept up in a four-horse carriage. They had an immense load of trunks, cases, and hat boxes. Julie curtsied to Dr. Bell and gave me a fleeting, but winsome smile. Penelope gave me a cold look of complete disdain and walked away without a greeting. Did she still blame me for the death of her German lover, Count von Wittenberg, when we were in Russia? She hadn't been upset when he died and had even run off with the Prince of Wales that same afternoon! Perhaps she was disappointed that I had not stayed in touch with her when she was having her dalliance with the prince. As always, though, she was the one who had left — not I. Why would she be angry with me?

As we settled on board, I followed our familiar travel ritual — first suggested by Dr. Bell years ago — and chewed ginger root to ward off the mal de mer that I suffered during our first passage to America. When tugs pushed the *Oregon* away from her dock, the band struck up "Heart of Oak" and then the rather mournful "Navy Hymn." I spent a splendid afternoon watching the flats and low hills of Liverpool Harbor, but when the ship turned south at Anglesey Island, I reluctantly went to our stateroom.

A handsome, black steward in a resplendent white uniform had put our clothing away in the spacious closet. He and Dr. Bell chatted as if they were old friends. "Arthur, meet Samuel Wallace. He has news of Rufus," Dr. Bell said. I was all ears. Rufus had been our steward during our first passage to America and became our friend and all-purpose assistant who helped identify the culprits in a scheme to assassinate the U.S. president. Security demands that I should not mention in public, how we foiled the assassination. The details remain secure in my diary. Rufus, a black man, had been uneducated, but proved himself on that trip to be smart and skilled. He dreamed of becoming a doctor and help people around the world. With Dr. Bell's influence, Rush Medical College in Chicago had accepted Rufus.

Samuel grinned and showed a row of impeccable white teeth. "Ah knowed Rufus as 'Bub' when we worked together for a time on the *Servia*. He was ma best fren' and he tol' me about how you fixed those Rebs. He be Dr. Rufus Freeman now an' done hung out his shingle in Memphis. I's right proud of him." Though not surprised, I was delighted to hear that Rufus was accomplishing his dream.

Samuel efficiently put away our clothing, stacked books on the shelves, and arranged toilet articles in the bathroom. When he was about to take his leave, Dr. Bell put a gold coin in his hand. Samuel flinched and held his wrist. "Ah got this swellin' that hurts when ah uses ma hands," he said.

There was an egg-sized lump on the back of his right wrist. "That is a ganglion, also known as a synovial cyst. I can cure it in a jiffy," said Dr. Bell.

"What you goin' to do?" asked Samuel.

"Sit here and place your hand and wrist flat on the desk. This will be quick."

Samuel clearly trusted Dr. Bell from all Rufus had said, and he plunked his hand down on the desk. "Now, close your eyes," said Dr. Bell. The good doctor ran his fingers over the swelling, made a minor adjustment in the placement of Samuel's hand and selected from the shelf a thick volume, *Lewis's Textbook of Surgery*. He hefted the book in both hands, then brought it down with great force and hit Samuel's wrist with a sharp *thwack!*

Samuel caught his breath, snatched his hand away, and looked at it in awe, as if it belonged to another person. "Glory, it be gone!" said he.

Dr. Bell applied a dab of menthol salve and wrapped a bandage around the wrist.

"There, all fixed; it will hurt for a day or so and then you will feel no pain," said Dr. Bell.

"I be always grateful to you doctors. Anything you need, just call on me," said Samuel.

When I went topside to catch a breath of fresh air, the ship was well down the Irish Sea, known to my ancestors by its true name, Muir Éireann. The wind was whistling in the rigging, and a nimble fellow — with a smart sailor's queue bound with a black ribbon that hung down the back of his neck — ran up the shrouds. He stood on one foot just beneath the very peak of the mainmast and sang out.

"Heave away, boys. Heave away."

A half dozen sailors sprang to the halyard and bent their backs to the work.

"Heave and haul, boys. Heave away."

"Our Davy says heave and haul away!" the sailors shouted. They stamped their feet and chanted louder. "Heave, heave!"

The sailor, Davy, high in the rigging, gave a merry shout. "Heave, you sailors, heave away!"

I thought of my pleasant months on board the *Hope*, while whaling in the high Arctic, and wanted to leap to the rigging to chant with these good sailors and experience, once again, the camaraderie of a crew sailing together. Instead, I scribbled their cries in my notebook so as not to forget the experience.

Heave and haul away, you say.
Our Davy says heave and haul away!
Down we haul. Down with the Queen's knickers!

The chant continued as the great sail rose and caught the wind. The sailors laughed while doing their work. Davy, way up in the rigging, seemed to be a favorite among the sailors and a natural leader. I envied him his freedom.

A glaring, short, squat, red-faced fellow with the stripe of a petty officer swaggered up a ladder to the deck. "Damn you, Davy! Damn your lazy hide. Enough of that tomfoolery. Get down and help haul on that halyard!" the man shouted.

"Right-O," replied the sailor. He grabbed a line and, fast as a bullet, slid down the rope, facing the mast and away from the cluster of men. A gust of wind caught him and the rope just before he reached the deck. His feet struck the petty officer's shoulder, knocking him to the deck. With a dancer's grace, Davy landed on his feet and, before joining the other sailors in their work, offered his hand to the fallen officer, who smacked it away. The petty officer rose from the deck, glowering with rage.

"Damn! You struck me! Smashed my shoulder on purpose. It's the brig for you; stupid sod!"

The men slowly and deliberately cleated the halyard and turned on the officer. "It war' an accident and you ain't hurt," growled a huge sailor. Davy, their leader, clenched his fists.

"Oh, it is mutiny you want? Right, then!" screamed the officer. I watched with utter amazement as the man drew a revolver, took deliberate aim, and fired a single shot. Davy grabbed his upper leg, but bright red blood spurted over the deck and down his leg. He collapsed on the deck.

" All of you, back to work!" shouted the petty officer.

The other sailors shrank away and went back to toiling with the halyards. I bounded forth, removed the blue bandana from the fallen sailor's neck, made a compress, and jabbed it into the wound. I put all my weight on the wound until the bleeding slowed to a trickle. The bullet must have severed his femoral artery in the groin. He had lost at least a pint of blood, though Davy neither screamed nor groaned but forced a smile as he looked up at me. "Thankee," he said.

I had not noticed before, but at my side, there appeared a smallish fellow with a full beard cut square across. "He is a brave man and you saved his life," he said.

"He will live if we can stop the hemorrhage," I said.

"Sad. So sad. Petty officers can be so cruel to hardworking, honest sailors," said he.

It seemed to be an eternity before the captain and the first officer appeared to restore order. "Quiet! You and you, take this man to sick bay. The rest of you — to your quarters," commanded the first officer.

The sick bay, with an examining room and five beds, was bright and clean. A woman with tightly-coiled blond hair and wearing a long, grey dress buttoned to the neck, was behind a desk. "Send for the ship's surgeon. This man has been shot. The femoral artery is bleeding," said I.

The woman sat straighter and glared. "I am Dr. Maude Topenham, the ship's surgeon," she said.

I was taken aback and momentarily released pressure from the wound. A geyser of blood erupted from the wound and splashed on the wall and floor. I leaned in to the job again until the bleeding stopped and composed myself. "I apologize, ma'am. I thought you were a nurse," said I.

"I have a medical degree from the Woman's Medical College of Pennsylvania." The woman doctor — I can't say she was a lady — rose from her chair. She was tall and not unattractive, but neither was she appealing. Her skirt swished as she went to the wounded sailor and felt his pulse at the wrist. "Pshaw, there is no need for surgery. Echinacea powder and a tight bandage is all he needs. A one-in-a-thousand dilution of Cinchona will prevent a fever," she said.

Sailors were lurking at the door, wondering about their fellow crew member. "Call for the captain and Dr. Joseph Bell. Run for it!" I shouted. Captain Cottier arrived a moment before Dr. Bell and took in the situation at a glance. My arms were bloody to the elbows and there was a scarlet splatter on the wall. The captain had most likely been in the service during the days when officers treated sick sailors and performed rough surgery.

"This is no case for homeopathy. Dr. Joseph Bell is one of the world's foremost surgeons. We shall let him decide." said the captain.

The good professor, with Samuel trailing behind carrying the instrument case, hurried into the room. He scarcely glanced at the woman doctor and took charge. She had a hand across her bosom. A look of malignant hatred crossed her features, and she then broke into a stiff smile. "I shall happily offer my services," she said.

Dr. Topenham bustled about, getting in the way, until an orderly — a wizened little fellow with bright, intelligent eyes — arranged clean towels and basins for the carbolic antiseptic solution. "Henry Burns, at your service. I can administer the chloroform if you wish," said he.

"How very kind," said Dr. Bell. We soaked the instruments in a carbolic solution, cleaned the skin, and set to work. The fumes of chloroform rose from the folded towel over the patient's face. Bell slashed through the sailor's clothing with a curved bistoury. "Samuel, press here with all your weight." Dr. Bell indicated the right lower quadrant of the patient's abdomen. I understood immediately. Pressure on the iliac artery would stop the hemorrhage while we searched for the femoral artery. It is an important surgical principle to have proximal control of a bleeding vessel. The scene could have been a surgical demonstration at the medical school. Dr. Bell rolled up his sleeves while I removed my blood-stained coat. We soaked our hands in the carbolic, and Dr. Bell selected his sharpest scalpel and incised the skin above and below the bullet wound just under the crease that separates the upper thigh from the abdomen. I recited to myself to ensure I was accurately considering the anatomical details. *The femoral artery emerges from beneath the inguinal ligament about halfway between the pubis and the iliac spine and enters Hunter's canal over the sartorius muscle just medial to the femoral nerve.* There it was, the femoral artery, with a ragged hole. Without pausing, Dr. Bell passed stout ligatures around the artery above and below the wound. He mopped up a blood clot and wiped the area with a solution of carbolic.

"Samuel, please release the pressure," said he. There was no more bleeding. I heaved a sigh of relief, but we were not finished. Dr. Bell removed bits of clothing and plunged a forceps into the tract of the bullet. "Ah, there it is, embedded in the femur." He worked the forceps up and down and then extracted the smashed bullet. "I fear the femur is cracked. Doyle, if you please, stitch the wound and apply a Thomas splint to immobilize the leg," Dr. Bell said.

After he packed his instruments, and with a slight bow to Dr. Topenham, Dr. Bell took his leave.

Davy came out of the anaesthetic without a whimper, thanks to the skill of Henry Burns. Burns again demonstrated his ability by applying the Thomas splint, a clumsy contraption of a padded ring and steel rods to the injured leg.

"You have had medical training," said I.

"A year at Guy's, but the book learning was above me. I could nae pass the examinations" said Burns.

Dr. Topenham had taken her small bag and left sick bay. "She goes to make her rounds of the women this time o' day," said Burns.

"Why does the ship have a woman doctor?" I asked.

" 'Tis a sad tale. The last doctor was a good man, a kindly man, but he mixed laudanum with drink until he went daft. They carried him off the ship in a straightjacket to a hospital in Boston. The lady doctor was the only one available at the last minute. The captain signed her on for the last voyage and so, here we are," said Burns.

"Can she perform surgery?" I asked.

"She claims to be a natural healer. I admit, she is good with women troubles but not much else."

I pondered this state of affairs and was happy to leave a capable man like Burns in charge of our patient. "Give him a light diet and no more than a teaspoon of laudanum for pain," I said.

I left and took a turn around the promenade deck, glancing into the ladies' drawing room as I passed, hoping to see Julie. The room was beautifully appointed and furnished in the costliest manner. I spied Penelope at a damask-covered table; an empty glass was by her elbow. She held a Sobranie Black Russian cigarette between her second and third fingers. Smoke curled upwards towards the ceiling when she exhaled through her nose. She was as I remembered her — a modern, sophisticated woman. My mam would say she was 'a bad un' and should nae be trusted,' but I couldn't stifle a feeling of yearning to spend time with her.

"May I join you?" I asked. She gave me a sour glance, that turned, in a moment, to a lovely smile. She put the cigarette to her lips and took in a lungful of smoke as she eyed me from head to toe. There were fine wrinkles around her eyes, something I had never noticed before. She exhaled a cloud of acrid smoke.

"If you wish," said she.

"Would you care for a drink?"

"Yes."

I ordered two of the new 'cocktails,' brandy with a dash of Angostura bitters and lemon.

I tapped my fingers on the table. We remained silent until the drinks arrive.

"Are you working for Her Majesty again?" I asked.

She tossed her head, and I caught a whiff of orange blossoms, her favorite scent. "I had no choice. My father drank up his inheritance and no longer has any influence. Prince Bertie turned out to be a fat playboy and I lost interest." She snuffed out the cigarette and downed her drink. "I may settle in America and marry a rich man."

She gave me one of her most radiant smiles. My heart skipped a beat or two when she then leaned forward and caressed my hand. She was still beautiful.

"Order another drink," said she.

"Only if you allow me to escort you to dinner."

"Yes, but aren't you really interested in Miss Pembroke?" she teased.

"Oh, dear Penelope, Julie is a patient," said I.

It was nearly time for the first gala dinner at sea when I left Penelope to change into proper attire. Oh, the luxury of a first-class stateroom. Just think — we had our very own bath. I had a hot soak and then dressed for dinner. I cursed the links and studs but managed the starched shirt and winged collar before struggling into my waistcoat, which fit perfectly. Dr. Bell was resplendent in his usual black, velvet, Barathea jacket, a tartan waistcoat, and his dress blue kilt. He was indeed a noble Scotsman. "The captain invited me to dine at his table this evening. I must do justice to our great city," said he.

Edison electric lights flooding the Grand Salon set the gold and white ceiling decorations and the satinwood, paneled walls to glowing. The first-class passengers were already tapping their feet in tune with the string orchestra, and swigging down cocktails. Dr. Bell immediately went off to find the captain's table, while I wandered in the crowd until I caught a whiff of orange blossoms and spied Penelope. At that moment, I forgave all of her sins and the way she had repeatedly lured me in and then rejected me. She was absolutely bewitching in a frothy green, satin gown that revealed delicious, creamy shoulders and enough bosom to set my heart beating faster. I was about to proudly take her arm and escort her to a table when a handsome chap, in red trousers and a dark blue jacket, bowed low and kissed her hand. I had pangs of jealousy until Julie Pembroke came out of the crowd, diverting my attention, and offered me her hand. I bent and caressed her dainty fingers with my lips. She rewarded me with a beatific smile. In light of Penelope's dismissal, I was especially grateful for her kindness and attention and could have instantly fallen in love, except that the companion to the cad who had swept away my dear Penelope came over and bowed to Julie.

"Shall we make up a foursome?" The fellow had an American accent, a carefully trimmed mustache, and rather long, sandy-colored hair. He was as elegant as any British toff. He swept her away, leaving me feeling like the lower-class working man I am. I guess it just confirms that I must get my doctorate and join the upper classes. I slunk away and took a seat at the dinner table next to a heavy-set gentleman with curly, dark red hair flecked with grey, and an enormous mustache. There was what appeared to be a scar, like an old rope burn, on the back of his neck.

"I am Arthur Conan Doyle." The man rose and made a sweeping bow.

"Colonel Ned Buntline, at your service," he said.

"Do you have business in the States?" I asked.

"Business? Great Jehoshaphat, no. Business is for those poor fools with no imagination. I write stories and entertain the public. Why, sir, I have just arranged a show starring Buffalo Bill Cody to take place in London. Damn it all, it is time for the Europeans to learn about the real Wild West of America," said Mr. Buntline.

We took our seats, and after partaking of a glass of very fine wine, I resumed our conversation. "I have heard of this Buffalo Bill. Wasn't he an Indian scout on the Great Plains?" I asked.

He glared at me for a long moment. "Hell's Bells! Haven't you read my story, *Buffalo Bill, King of the Border Men?*"

"No sir, but I have a great interest in writing, though there is little money in such an endeavor," said I.

"No money? Damn it all, you can make a fortune, boy. Why, I can dash off a story in one afternoon that will sell for thousands of dollars."

I nearly fell over. Most writers had complained of poverty and advised me not to try my hand at writing. "You must have a secret." .

"Hell no. Every great story has romance, a dastardly deed, and revenge. Start with a cowboy — let's call him Slim — who is in love with the boss's daughter. He is poor, but honest, and has no chance with the girl until a gang of desperados murders her father and kidnaps her. The leader of the gang is one of the best gunfighters in the west, but Slim leaps on his horse and gives chase all by himself. He kills all the gang with his trusty six-shooter and, even when shot and bleeding, he knocks out the gunfighter with his bare fists. He rescues the girl and collects a ten-thousand-dollar reward. He gets the girl and the ranch. It is a sure-fire formula."

I plied Mr. Buntline with questions while I indulged in the meal's multiple courses. It was after the oysters, when I was spooning clear consommé, that the frosty dowager across the table gave me a cutting look and spoke to me sotto voce, though it could be heard around the table. "Young man, you are using the spoon intended for cream soup." How was I to know the difference? My face became hot, and as the meal continued, I watched how everyone else at the table ate and focused on my food in order to avoid her further judgement. I had grilled lobster, beef steak, roast pheasant, lamb with mint sauce, creamed peas, a sorbet, buttered new potatoes, fresh asparagus, pâté de foie gras, and, at last, peaches in jelly with a chocolate éclair. I surreptitiously undid the top button of my trousers, which had grown tight after indulging in the delicious food, and woefully looked across the salon.

Julie was in animated conversation with the American gentleman. The fellow in red trousers alongside Penelope must have told a joke, because Julie giggled and then laughed out loud. The only jokes I knew were mostly anatomical and wouldn't do in mixed company. Just before we rose from the dinner table, Mr. Buntline clapped his hand on my shoulder. "Remember ... the bad man always wears a black hat and carries a gun on each hip."

After an hour or so in the smoking room with a fine cigar and more than one brandy, I went, unsteadily, out on deck and leaned against the railing for a breath of salt air. After a few moments, Dr. Bell appeared out of the gloom. "It is a fine night," he said.

"Yes, indeed, the stars are brilliant."

"I am worried about that boy's leg. Let us visit sick bay," said Dr. Bell.

Henry Burns' head was down on folded arms on the desk; he snored softly and smelled of beer. I nudged his arm. He came awake with a start and rubbed his sleepy eyes. "How is our patient?" I asked.

"Right as rain, sir, right as rain. I shall switch on the Edison lights so's you can see for yourself."

Davy was dead white. His lifeless body was still warm and showed no sign of rigor mortis. Dr. Bell quickly examined the body. "He has not been dead for more than an hour. There is no sign of bleeding or gangrene," said he.

There was nothing amiss that I could see. "Perhaps he had a delayed reaction to the anaesthetic," I said.

Dr. Bell continued his examination. "What is this?" he exclaimed.

"I see nothing untoward," said I.

"Come, lad, the pupils of the eye become widely dilated just before death and remain fixed in position."

I looked more closely at the open eyes. "Yes, yes, now, I see. His pupils are about halfway between pinpoint and normal," I said.

"Does that suggest anything to you?" asked Dr. Bell.

"An opiate, such as morphine, produces pinpoint pupils."

"Mr. Burns, did the patient move at all after we left?" asked Dr. Bell.

"Oh, no, sir. The splint kept him immobile, just as you ordered," said Burns.

"Did you pull his under sheet tight?" asked Dr. Bell.

"Yes, sir, tight as a drum, it was, hospital-like," said Burns.

Dr. Bell's questioning of the little man made no sense. I was puzzled, and Burns quivered under Dr. Bell's unrelenting gaze. "Were you with him all evening?" asked Bell.

"I slipped out for a bite of supper and some refreshment wi' the port watch," Mr. Burns said.

"Has Dr. Topenham been here?"

"Oh no, sir. The doctor takes her meals in her quarters and retires early unless she has to visit a sick passenger."

"I gather she treats the passengers in their rooms and sees the crew here in sick bay?"

"That is correct, sir."

"Now, Arthur, a bit of sleuthing. Is there anything unusual about the bed?" asked Dr. Bell. I looked closely and remembered that Burns said he had made the bottom sheet 'drum tight' like a proper hospital bed, yet there were wrinkles on the bottom sheet.

"If the patient was completely immobile, how did he wrinkle the bottom sheet next to him?" I asked.

"Very perceptive," Dr. Bell said. He traced the wrinkled sheet with his index finger. Was it my imagination, or had he outlined a vague impression of a human form?

"Mr. Burns, see to the body. I shall request a captain's investigation of the death," said Dr. Bell.

Despite a fogged brain, I sat up until the wee hours of the morning, setting down every detail of this day. I am counting on the idea that my compulsion to write and record everything, especially the expertise of Dr. Bell, will provide fodder for my novel.

31 May 1883, at sea

The inquest was a farce. Dr. Topenham testified that the patient died as a result of our unnecessary surgical meddling and anaesthetic shock. The captain ignored my eye-witness account of the shooting, as well as that of the small, bearded gentleman who was on deck at the time. "My officer enforced discipline and prevented a mutiny," said the captain. I left the hearing with my bearded friend, and together, we strolled aft on the promenade deck. We leaned on the railing and watched the small white-capped waves driven by a gentle northeast breeze.

"My name is Arthur Conan Doyle." The bearded gentleman languidly shook my hand and offered an absentminded smile.

"Herman Melville," he said.

"The author of *Typee* and *Moby Dick*?"

"The very same," said he.

"Sir, I have read your books. They are remarkable adventures! I have looked for more, but it seems you have written nothing during the past few years. Is that so?"

"So, young man, have you really read my stories?"

"Yes sir, every word."

His kindly face was sad. "The critics said I was mad, totally mad. In Boston, the clergy burned my books."

"I would give up medicine if I could write half as well as you."

"No, don't give writing a moment's thought. Medicine is an honorable profession. Writing only leads to poverty. I can write about sailing men and sailing ships, but the age of sail is almost over. Now the poor fellows are in a dark, steel cage shoveling coal instead of up there in the rigging enjoying a fresh breeze and sunshine," said he.

"Yes, I understand. I have traveled on multiple ships and even served as ship's surgeon on an arctic whaler. The conditions were often terrible, but the men had a fair life. They were cruel to the animals, however."

"The life of a sailor can be brutal. On one of my ships, the second mate falsely accused a topsail man, named Billy, of thievery. The captain ordered a hundred lashes. Of course, the poor fellow died. Yesterday's episode reminded me of poor Billy.

"Why not write a story about him?" I asked.

"Perhaps, someday."

We pushed through the crowd to the bar. Mr. Melville ordered brandy and water while I, still feeling the effects of last night, had a lemon squash. In the far corner of the room, Penelope and Julie played whist with their escorts of the night before. Penelope was partnered with the American this time, and the bounder was fondling her knee. I could not help but stare, with more than a twinge of jealousy. But for which girl did I feel more? Julie was ravishing and appeared to be under the spell of the damned fellow who had swept her away from me last night.

A fellow nudged my elbow. "A couple of lovely dishes, eh?" He had a pleasant twinkle. "Giles Stevens of the London Times," he said.

"Pleased to make your acquaintance. I am Arthur Doyle and this is Mr. Herman Melville, the great author." Mr. Stevens toyed with his drink and stared across the room with a hungry look.

"Look at them — a damn Russian and an American with the two best looking women on the ship," he said.

After my escapades in St. Petersburg, I was interested in anything Russian. "I didn't realize that the other man was Russian. Who is he?" I asked.

"Count Nikolai Borovsky, a distant cousin to the new tsar. He was a director of the Russian-American Company before they sold out to the Americans," said Stevens.

"So, this Borovsky must be wealthy," I said.

"In the early days, the Russians made a fortune in furs, but they fell on hard times. Borovsky was more interested in minerals, and he may have swindled the company before Russia sold Alaska to the Americans," said Stevens.

"Who is the American?" I asked. "Not certain, but he claims to be a California mining engineer and I believe I heard someone address him as Mr. Dawson."

Our little group broke up, and I whiled away a half hour or so attempting to learn the game of whist, but it was no use. After a time, I wandered into the library to search for the book by Henry James, *Principles of Whist Stated and Explained*. Dr. Bell was there surrounded by books and stacks of newspapers. "Laddie, I am troubled by that boy's death. It reminded me of a brief note in the London papers about a series of mysterious deaths in Boston." He pushed a month's worth of the *Boston Herald* across the table. "Look for reports of unusual deaths, especially in young men."

This is one of the Doctor's methods for solving mysteries. He is convinced that criminals repeat their crimes and the solution is always to find a common thread. I didn't expect to find anything, but set to work looking through the stack of papers. There were long stories about the completion of the Brooklyn Bridge and the end of the spoils system in politics. I read about the man named Buffalo Bill — who Colonel Buntline had mentioned was organizing a Wild West of America show — and about a telephone line connecting New York with Chicago.

I grew tired and was struggling to focus when a story in the paper from the twentieth of April caught my eye. It was about a young man who died in a nursing home after a trivial injury. It happened in Quincy, a city not far from Boston. An attendant had found the young man dead in bed, and an unidentified doctor pronounced the death as due to a fractured tibia and a shock to his nervous system. I had seen a number of fractures of the tibia, but had never known of that causing a death. I read the story to Dr. Bell.

"It may mean nothing, but I don't believe in coincidences. Arthur, here is your chance to use your wits. Why should a young, healthy man such as the one in the Quincy nursing home or Davy die after a trivial injury?" Dr. Bell asked.

"Perhaps, a sudden stoppage of the heart or a stroke," said I.

"Oh, stuff and nonsense! Think, man. Use your training. Observe, deduce, and connect. Remember the pupils of his eyes." I thought hard. There had been no signs of distress, no contortion of Davy's limbs to suggest a fit. His face was peaceful in death.

"Some sort of poison," said I.

"Close ... Have you heard the expression, 'in the arms of Morpheus'?"

"Yes, an overdose of morphine would cause a peaceful death and explain the near pinpoint pupils of his eyes. But who could have administered the fatal dose?" I asked.

"I first suspected Mr. Burns, but in the annals of crime, women are just as likely to be serial killers as men. Deranged killers, such as Jack the Ripper, combine a longing with hatred for the opposite sex."

"But why? I asked.

"Disturbed sexuality," replied Bell.

"Only two people would have had access to a supply of morphine — Mr. Burns and Dr. Topenham. If the death in Quincy is related, it could not have been Burns because he was on the ship at the time," I said.

"There, you have it. Dr. Topenham came on the ship in Boston after the Quincy murder. We must set a trap to catch her and be sure she is the killer. I shall leave that to you," said Bell. I felt pleased that Dr. Bell was giving me responsibility in solving the case.

I was preparing for dinner with Penelope when Samuel entered with fresh towels. "Mr. Arthur, you dasn't go to dinner with dat bristly face. You jes set still, right here, and I will give you the best shave of your life," said the steward. I relaxed under the steaming towel until he brushed on foaming lather and, with all the deftness of a surgeon, gently passed a wicked straight razor over my face. "Now, this here lotion is goin' to make you feel like a million dollars," said Samuel. He slapped on a fragrant lotion and rubbed until my skin fairly glowed.

"That feels wonderful. What is it?" I asked.

"Dat's bay rum. Folks down in the islands soaks mashed up fresh bay leaves in Jamaica rum and add a little lemon and orange," he said.

I whistled on my way to their stateroom. If fortune smiled on me, even if Penelope continued to rebuff my romantic attentions, I might end up whirling Julie around the dance floor after dinner. As I arrived, daydreaming of dancing in Julie's arms, she opened the door to my knock and, to my shock, immediately clutched her throat, rolled back her eyes, and went absolutely rigid. She appeared to be in a deep hypnotic trance. "Penelope, bring Dr. Bell! This instant, please!" I shouted. I led Julie to a chair. She sat down, but appeared to have no awareness of her surroundings.

Dr. Bell arrived and, in his usual manner, first listened to my story and intently observed the girl. His concentration was uncanny. I explained the abrupt onset of her trance when she had opened the door. As I spoke, Julie remained quiet and rigid. Her eyes were half open but clearly sightless. She made no response to questions nor appeared to hear any sounds we made, such as clapping our hands.

"Arthur, please leave the room for at least five minutes," said Dr. Bell. I was totally mystified, but did as he ordered. I lingered on the deck for five minutes by my watch and re-entered the room. Julie was awake and seemed perfectly normal until the second I appeared. Her eyes rolled upwards, she went rigid, and was totally unresponsive.

"She knows you. The only change is that powerful scent. Charcot, the French neurologist has described a sort of self-hypnosis induced by smell," Dr. Bell said.

"Sir, is it possible to reach her mind when she is in the trance?" I asked.

"Let us make the attempt," said Dr. Bell. He knelt by Julie, stroked her hand, and spoke softly as one would with a frightened child.

"Julie, dear, we are friends of Uncle Peachy. You are perfectly safe with us." There was a flicker of movement in her eyes.

"Julie, listen closely. Uncle Peachy wants to know about the man who visited Mildred. Did he smell nice?" Her hand jerked convulsively and she giggled with girlish amusement.

"You remember him. Was he amusing?" Dr. Bell asked. She giggled, then burst out laughing.

"He smells nice, but looks like a boiled egg. Oh, Milly, put it back," said Julie.

Dr. Bell stroked her arm and spoke in a soft, reassuring voice. "Julie, was he the same man who killed Mildred?" The poor girl went rigid. She clenched her eyes and, after a moment, shook violently.

"Must not bother Milly. Must not tell. Oh, Milly," she said.

"A small mirror, please," said Dr. Bell. Penelope produced a mirror from her purse. Dr. Bell adjusted the electric lamp and repeatedly reflected bright flashes of light from the mirror into Julie's eyes.

There was no response until she batted at her face. "Bright, too bright," said she. Suddenly she burst into tears. "Oh, where is my sister? Has the awful man left?"

"You are safe. You smelled a scent, but it was only Arthur, not the man who was with Mildred," Dr. Bell said. She stretched and seemed disoriented, like someone coming out of a deep sleep.

"Why did the man look like a boiled egg?" Dr. Bell asked.

Her face again went blank. "I don't know," said Julie.

The evening was ruined. There would be no dinner and dancing. No hugging and kissing. Julie went from the quiet blankness to hysterical sobbing to pacing the floor. Penelope agreed to watch over her for the night.

It is now much later and I am about to collapse into bed, leaving Dr. Bell puffing his favorite meerschaum pipe and frowning in deep concentration.

1 June 1883, at sea on the *Oregon*

Giles Stevens, the London Times reporter, is in his early thirty's, not a young man, and he limps on a trick knee. We were enjoying a rasher of bacon, poached eggs, kippered herring, and an assortment of pastries. The tea was first rate. "Giles, would you like a bit of excitement and to help solve a crime?" I asked.

He wiped egg from his chin. "Only if it involves good-looking women."

"You will be bait to catch a killer and, yes, a woman is involved, but I would wager she is not your type."

"I smell a story. Do I get an exclusive if we catch the killer?"

"Of course. You can leave us out of it. Dr. Bell loathes the press."

Mr. Stevens didn't need to put on an act. His knee was truly painful. He hobbled into sick bay groaned at the approach of Dr. Topenham. She made a cursory examination, prescribed a harmless homeopathic remedy, and ordered Mr. Burns to bandage the knee. "Stay in bed. I will visit you this evening to make quite certain you are comfortable," said Dr. Topenham. Giles put on a realistic display of his disability and put his arm over my shoulder for support. With my support, he limped to the lounge for a much-needed brandy.

"Giles, if this Dr. Topenham is indeed the killer, you may be in danger. She must be incredibly clever to get away with murder. Are you certain you want to go through with this?" I asked.

"I have been in danger before. Never fear," said Giles.

"I admire your bravery, but still, I will have Samuel, the steward, look after you. Take care."

A few hours later, I met Mr. Melville for a stroll on deck. We paused to admire the ship's arrow-straight wake and her trail of black smoke. "Fast and more reliable, but not as romantic as a sailing ship," I said.

Melville shaded his eyes and peered over the sea, which sparkled in the bright sunshine, as if he were on the lookout for a whale. I expected him to shout, "Thar she blows!" Instead, to my surprise, he cried out something far different. "Man overboard!" he shouted, and pointed to a small body entangled in a rope ladder that dangled over the side. Within seconds, a sailor threw out a life ring, a whistle blew, and the ship's engines shuddered and shut down. Officers and a crowd of spectators swarmed to the rail. The bosun's mates lowered a boat. The sailors cut away the tangle of ropes and, within minutes, hoisted the boat with its dreadful cargo.

Death is a failure for every doctor, perhaps more so to a newly minted physician like me. Even though I have seen cadavers in medical school, and witnessed several deaths when we were last in America and in Russia, I couldn't help but choke back bile when I pressed my fingers to her ice cold neck. I had not expected a pulse and there was none. Even the faintest flutter of her carotid artery would have meant life. Julie was dead. She wore only a light nightdress, which was half off her shoulders. I covered her with my jacket. Even in death, Julie was beautiful. I couldn't stomach the thought of my patient and potential love being dead and barely made it to the rail before heaving bile into the ocean.

"Davy was meant to haul up the ladder after the pilot left," said the bosun. "After he was shot, it was never done."

"But then, had the ladder been lifted, she would have disappeared without a trace," said Mr. Melville.

The first officer supervised transfer of the body to sick bay. Bad news spreads quickly. Dr. Bell arrived immediately and watched Dr. Topenham perform a cursory examination.

"The woman was addled by drink and fell overboard. It was a simple accident," she said.

"You must perform an autopsy," said Dr. Bell.

"No need to disturb the passengers," said the first officer. "The captain would never approve such a thing. She obviously drowned."

Dr. Bell flicked open his penknife and, with one motion, made an incision down the center of Julie's neck. The first officer lunged forward, but I smashed my fist into his face. He staggered back, blood pouring out of his nose. "Damn you!" He lurched forward, but I blocked him with a kick to his knee that dropped him to the floor.

"Arthur, stop the fisticuffs and assist me. Mr. Burns, two small retractors, if you please," said Dr. Bell.

Burns opened a glass-fronted case and secured two small retractors, instruments with a sharp hook on the end to hold open wounds. Bell made a precise incision that opened the trachea. I inserted the hooks into the wind pipe and pulled it open. It was empty. Dr. Bell pushed gauze down the wind pipe. It was perfectly dry.

"There is no water in her windpipe. Miss Pembroke was dead before she entered the water," said Dr. Bell.

"Is it a case of murder?" I asked.

"We shall see about that," said Dr. Bell.

Dr. Topenham, with her hand over her mouth, rushed out of sick bay.

"Arrest that woman!" I said.

"Not so fast, laddie. Let her be for now. She was most likely taken with a sudden nausea."

I had expected Dr. Bell to demand a full autopsy, but he merely proceeded to a methodical examination of the body. There were no bruises, wounds, or other signs of violence. Dr. Bell filled his meerschaum pipe with Cavendish, lit up, and blew a cloud of smoke. After a full five minutes of silent contemplation, he withdrew a small magnifying glass from its case and minutely examined dear Julie's face. "There! Arthur, look carefully. There is a shallow indentation on her cheek to the right of her mouth and minute indentations on the left side. The killer placed a hand over her mouth and, with his thumb and forefinger, choked off her nose," said Dr. Bell.

"Someone with a strong hand suffocated her and then threw the body overboard," I said, feeling the bile again rising in my throat.

"Exactly; but for the rope ladder, she would have disappeared, leaving no evidence that she was murdered."

"Would the handprint show in a photograph?" I asked.

"If we arrange the light correctly," Dr. Bell replied.

I hastened to get my equipment. Mr. Burns focused the lights. I took several photographs that, later demonstrated an unmistakable outline of a hand — the hand that choked the life out of dear, sweet Julie. I was determined to bring the killer to justice with my own bare hands. I had dreamed of holding her in my arms and kissing those soft lips that were now cold and dead. She hadn't hurt anyone. Why would someone murder dear Julie? While mourning the fact that I would never be able to be with her, I suddenly remembered Penelope. Was she in danger as well? I couldn't bear to experience another loss, so I ran up a ladder and forward to their stateroom on the promenade deck. Thankfully, Penelope opened the door, though she was still in night clothing. Her eyes drooped with fatigue, and her hair was disheveled.

"Julie is dead," said I.

Her expression hardly changed, but her hand shook as she lit a Sobranie cigarette. She flicked out the lucifer and sat with a bare leg crossed over her knee. "Julie was hysterical until quite late, then she slept for an hour or so. I watched over her until nearly dawn. She felt better and went out for air. I finally fell asleep," said Penelope.

Could I believe her? Penelope had been a double agent. I wanted to trust her, to believe she would not lie again — especially to me — but I couldn't be sure. Was she loyal to the Crown or was she working with an enemy to England? Did she care about Julie, or was this just pretense?

Later, in our stateroom, I put the question to Dr. Bell. "Did one killer commit both murders?"

"No, the methods are completely different. The sailor died with an overdose of morphine. Whoever killed Julie had an entirely different motive."

"Could the same person have killed both twins?" I asked.

"Yes, the methods were different, but the killer must have had a motive to be rid of the twins," Dr. Bell said.

"What about Penelope? Could she have committed both crimes to put us off the scent?" I asked.

"No, Penelope is devious, but not a cold-blooded killer. In fact, we must combine forces with her to find a man who looks like a boiled egg," said Dr. Bell.

"Come, now, it must be a silly joke," said I.

"It came from her subconscious. Julie told the truth. The killer is bald. He must have an excellent toupee. We must look for a gentleman who brushes his hair the exact same way every day," said Dr. Bell.

I rang for Samuel. He arrived promptly. "Samuel, be a good fellow and invite Lady Walshingham to our quarters for tea," I said. Penelope arrived and took the tea but waved away the scones and jam.

Dr. Bell went right to the point. "Do you have any thoughts on who could have murdered Julie?" he asked.

"Colonel Beachy-Edwards is investigating a plot against England that involves the Pacific coast of Canada. Mildred obtained information for him during a tryst. The killer naturally would have thought that Julie had overheard him speak in a moment of passion," said Penelope.

"Do you suspect anyone?" asked Dr. Bell.

"There are dozens of Americans on this ship. Could be any one of them," she said.

"What about that Dawson fellow?" I asked. She waved off my question with an enigmatic smile and abruptly went her way.

2 June 1883, at sea

I met Giles at breakfast. He walked with an exaggerated limp but appeared to be cheerful. "Giles, what happened?" I asked.

He slathered a bit of toast with marmalade. "The nice lady doctor arrived just before midnight, enquired about my health, and left a small dose of laudanum. She was very solicitous. You medical blokes could take lessons from her in bedside manners."

"Look sharp," I said.

The ship's officers soothed the passengers' fears by claiming that Julie had fallen overboard accidently. She was quickly forgotten because everyone was more focused on placing bets on the exact day and hour of our arrival in Boston. Dr. Bell spent the day working on his textbook of surgery while I strolled the deck and occasionally looked in on the game room where Penelope avidly played whist with Borovsky the Russian, Dawson the American, and a bejeweled dowager. I studied the game and was still confused by the strict rules of bidding, tricks, and trumps. Dawson appeared to have an eye disorder since he blinked, winked, and raised his eyebrows from time to time. Periodically, Penelope swept a pile of banknotes off the table.

3 June 1883, at sea

For most people traveling by ship, one day is much like every other. The ship leaves a straight wake, passengers lounge on deck, and we all eat and drink too much. The English talk of troubles in Afghanistan, and the Americans chatter about horse races, politics, and the economic depression. No one mentioned the murders. The ship's officers have no leads, and at Dr. Bell's instruction, I have kept our plan a secret. If we do not catch the culprits soon, we will arrive in Boston and the killers will be free.

4 June 1883, at sea

Giles was remarkably cheerful. "You have it all wrong about the lady doctor."

"She may still kill you. Is Samuel keeping watch?" I asked.

"Oh yes. He fixed a comfortable spot for himself in a far corner of my stateroom."

I grumped about because the captain predicted we would dock in Boston a day earlier than expected — by noon tomorrow. This would be our last day and night at sea and we had not apprehended either killer. Dr. Bell seemed completely unconcerned. Dinner was again a sumptuous feast, and I overindulged on wine — at least that is my only explanation for my behavior later in the evening.

I can hardly write because my hand is swollen, and though I may have a broken carpal bone in my wrist, it is probably a mere sprain. Sometime after dinner, while many first-class passengers had crowded into the lounge for drinks, the dynamo failed and the Edison lights went out. Most passengers stumbled off to their staterooms. Penelope, the Russian, Borovsky, Dawson, and the same old dame, whose husband was apparently in the House of Lords, continued playing whist by gaslight. Penelope was partnered with Dawson, the American. I wanted to find the murderer, but also wanted a full night's sleep so we could start fresh again tomorrow. Dr. Bell sat his chair at our small table with his legs stretched out and his hands folded on his chest. A casual passerby would think that he was half asleep. He had not touched the tot of single malt whisky but raised a hooded eyebrow every time Dawson and Penelope won a trick.

"Arthur, what have you observed about the foursome?" he asked.

"Nothing in particular."

"Have I taught you nothing? Look closely. Dawson and Penelope are cheating."

"Do you mean the winks and raised eyebrows are some kind of a signal?" I asked.

"Of course," said Dr. Bell.

My mind whirled. Yes, Dawson! A man who cheats at cards is capable of any nefarious act, even murder. Before Dr. Bell could stop me, I sprinted across the room and caught the odor of bay rum. "Aha, it is you! Damn you!" I shouted. I snatched at Dawson's hair with all my might. He yelled. I yanked out a few hairs, but his coiffure was perfectly intact. Penelope pulled in a pile of banknotes and overturned the table on the Russian's lap. The count fell backwards but came to his feet with a growl. His locks of hair had become unhinged.

"No, YOU are the boiled egg!" I shouted at Borovsky.

He responded by lunging at my midsection. I went down, gasping for breath, but came up and smashed a haymaker into his face with my right fist. The Russian snatched a derringer from his pocket. "You dare to lay a hand on a nobleman!"

Penelope lifted her skirt with practiced ease, withdrew a small revolver from a holster on her ankle, and fired twice. The first bullet grazed the Russian's shoulder but the second struck dead center in his chest. The count groaned, clutched his chest, and theatrically collapsed on the floor. I ducked out of the way. Dawson rubbed his head, and the dowager remained perfectly calm, as if fisticuffs and gunplay were a regular occurrence. A blood stain rapidly spread over the Russian count's shirtfront, but he was very much alive. Dr. Bell calmly lifted the count's wig. His head did resemble a boiled egg. He inspected the wound and found that the low-powered .22 bullet had not penetrated the count's sternum. It was hardly more than a flesh wound.

Two ship's officers and the master-at-arms quickly took charge. "Take this man to sick bay and don't let him out of your sight. He may be a vicious killer," said Dr. Bell. He pulled me away from the excited group of passengers and officers. "Arthur, we must search his room. Be quick."

Off we went through darkened passageways until we halted at room 201. The professor jimmied the lock with a twisty surgical instrument suited for removing deep foreign bodies from wounds. "Strike a light," he said. By the light of a candle, we opened drawers, riffled through clothing, and searched a trunk. There was nothing unusual until Dr. Bell found a locked, red, leather case beneath the bed. He probed the lock until the lid sprung open to reveal small compartments filled with dozens of small stones wrapped in bits of paper. Each piece of paper had numbers written on it. We took one small, pale, white stone and a second, orange-colored bit of crystal wrapped in a paper with the numbers 62:48 132:12.

In sick bay, Mr. Burns had already removed the small bullet from the count's chest. The captain and first officer questioned the count and looked upon me with suspicion.

"You are under arrest for attacking a fellow passenger," said the captain.

"Sir, this man murdered Miss Pembroke."

"Bah, where is the proof?"

At this point, Count Borovsky put on a great show of bravado and innocence. "The fracas was all a mistake, a question of cards. I forgive the impetuous young man," said the Russian count.

Dr. Bell huddled with the captain. "We have evidence. Arthur, fetch the photographs, if you please," Dr. Bell said.

The dim outline of the hand in my photograph matched the count's. This might have been the first time in the history of crime detection that a photo incriminated a murderer, but it was not enough to convince the captain. He ordered the count to be confined to his room until officials in Boston could investigate.

I suddenly remembered Giles and had a terrible sense of foreboding. I confronted the first officer. "Come with me, quickly," I said.

We dashed down a flight of steps to the second-class section and, at the end of the corridor, found the door to Giles' room ajar. I will never forget the scene. Samuel, the steward, violently shook Giles who lay in a coma. "Wake up, wake up!" he screamed.

"What happened?" I shouted.

"I musta dozed off and thought it was a dream. De lady doctor was all sweet talk when she gave Mr. Giles a glass to drink. He took little sips, den a long pull, and sank back on the bed. She waited a minute or two, den lay down next to him, kissed his mouth and run her hand along his body. He groaned once or twice, like he was havin' a good time. I figured it warn't non o' my bizness. I lay quiet until I couldn' hep but sneeze. De lady doctor rised up and run right out of the room. Dat's when I figured somethin' was wrong."

Poor Giles was scarcely breathing. "Samuel, soapy water, quick! A pitcher of water with soap!" I cried.

Giles made automatic, feeble attempts to swallow when I poured the liquid into his mouth. Some went down his windpipe and he coughed. I pinched his skin and slapped his face until the soapy water worked. He vomited a gush of soapy water and emptied his stomach. At last, the poor fellow opened his eyes.

"Samuel, damn your hide . . . Coffee, a jug of hot, black coffee, now!" I shouted.

By the time daylight streamed through the porthole, Giles had finished the pot of coffee and walked with assistance. "Oh, what wonderful dreams; there were the sweetest lassies and wonderful kisses," said Giles. He sagged back on the bed. I shook him awake.

"What happened?" I asked.

"She was kind and so sweet. She gave me a drink of the most delightful medicine. I wanted more and more."

"You barely survived a lethal dose of morphine. Thank goodness you are alive! Now, you have a first-hand account and can tell the world how you helped identify — and survived — a serial killer," I said.

5 June 1883, Boston Harbor

The pilot boat met us as we drew near the Boston Light on Little Brewster Island. After the pilot boarded, the captain sent an urgent message on the returning boat, requesting police and an official from the British Consulate to meet the ship. The weather was glorious. Passengers crowded the deck to see the islands in Boston Harbor. The English hissed and booed when we steamed past the very spot where the rebels staged the Boston Tea Party. Horns tooted when tugs pushed the *Oregon* alongside Long Wharf in Boston Harbor. A dozen armed police held back a crowd of relatives and onlookers while excited passengers crowded against the railings. Everyone was thrilled to have been part of the record-breaking Atlantic crossing. The moment deck hands lowered the gangplank, I noticed Penelope, hand in hand with Jack Dawson, dash away and get lost in the crowd. I caught sight of them again, just as they entered a cab. Dawson carried the red, leather case that belonged to Count Borovsky. Penelope looked up at me, waved, and blew a kiss.

"This is not the last we will see of those two," said Dr. Bell. I felt a terrible pang. Why could it not have been Julie and me dashing away, hand in hand, to romance?

A ponderous, fattish, middle-aged man with woolly sideburns made his way up the gangplank. Despite a walking stick, he staggered as if he'd had a drink or two. A thin man with a bowler hat followed him. The second officer insisted that we accompany the two men to the captain's quarters. The captain offered tea, and we made introductions all around. The thin fellow was police detective William Kennedy. The fat man introduced himself. "Baron Sir Edmund Runcie, Her Majesty's Consulate."

The damn fellow was probably the worthless third son of a baron who found a place in the diplomatic corps, but he expected us to bow and scrape. Dr. Bell looked him over with his usual keen eyes. "Sir Edmund, you are not long from your posting in Hong Kong?"

"By jove, that is correct. Quite correct. We have never met. How did you know?"

"The rash on your face and your unsteady gait indicates an overdose of quinine. Hong Kong, of all the Crown Colonies is the worst for malaria. The carved dragon head on your walking stick is of Chinese origin," said Dr. Bell.

"By Jove, you are correct. Um, now, captain, you sent a message. Murders, eh? Do you have the scoundrels in custody?"

"We have no real proof that either death was a case of murder. There is only circumstantial medical evidence," said the captain.

"I proved the young woman was dead before she entered the water. A handprint on her face matches the hand of Count Borovsky, and there is an eyewitness for an attempted murder," said Dr. Bell.

Runcie twirled his mustache. "Borovsky, a Russian count, you say? Must not create an international incident with a false accusation." said he.

"You should also know that Dr. Topenham, the ship's doctor, may be a serial killer. Her case is one for the American police," I said.

"Where is this Dr. Topenham?" asked Detective Kennedy.

Captain Cottier turned to his first officer. "Well, is she in custody?" he asked.

"I am afraid, sir, that the ship's surgeon has disappeared. We have searched everywhere," the officer said.

"Damn! I will not stand for incompetence in my officers," Captain Cottier said.

"She is extremely clever," I said.

"Baron Runcie, Dr. Reginald Fitz at the Massachusetts General Hospital is a world renowned pathologist. I insist that he perform an autopsy on Julie Pembroke to prove she was murdered," said Dr. Bell.

"Oh, very well. Where is this Count Borovsky?" asked the pompous British consulate.

Two tough masters-at-arms brought in the manacled count. His nose was swollen and he favored his right shoulder. When introduced to the consulate, he bowed low.

"The Runcie line, a most noble family," said the count.

The damn British fool fairly beamed with pleasure. "I say, we must not manacle a nobleman. Will you be my guest, sir, until we resolve this unfortunate affair?"

Despite Dr. Bell's objections, the thing was settled. The consulate, a foppish British baron took Count Borovsky as if he were a visiting dignitary.

I loitered on deck. The first-class passengers continued disembarking in grand style to awaiting carriages, while the poor people in steerage shuffled by with their load of belongings wrapped in blankets or carried in small trunks. The women were dressed in long skirts, colorful blouses, shapeless cloaks, and bonnets. They all looked alike. It seemed hopeless. Dr. Topenham must have mingled with the steerage passengers and managed to disguise herself. I was growing anxious thinking she would go scot free and kill again, when I caught something amiss. I spotted a tallish, but stooped, woman who wore a ragged black shawl and a grey skirt that dragged on the deck. The hands of the lower-class women were red, rough, gnarled by hard work. Yet her hands, which clutched her shawl, were lily-white, and her fingers were clean and well tapered.

"Stop that woman!" I shouted, while pointing towards her. She heard my yell, pushed aside the other passengers, dashed down the gangplank, and disappeared in the crowd. I shouted for the police and set off after her but bumped into people at almost every step. It was no use. I caught a glimpse of her more than a block away. She crossed a main street, looked back to see if anyone was following her, and, in doing so, stumbled on the iron rail of a streetcar track and fell beneath the hooves of four dashing horses pulling a streetcar. It was indeed, Dr. Topenham. Her crushed head leaked brains onto the street. It was a dreadful death, but it had saved her from hanging, and she would never again be able to murder another innocent person.

In answer to Dr. Bell's urgent request, Professor Fitz, at Harvard agreed to perform the autopsy immediately. Samuel helped load our baggage into a two-horse cab and off we went. The driver, a loquacious Irish-American, drove slowly from one cobblestone street to another. He took great delight in pointing out the church where a fellow named Paul Revere hung lanterns and a hill where a band of farmers killed over a thousand British redcoats.

We at last arrived at the Massachusetts General Hospital facing the James River. Despite its pretentious dome and portico, it was not nearly as impressive as the Royal Edinburgh Infirmary. It was, however, famous in the medical world as being the place where ether was first used as an anaesthetic.

Reginald Fitz was a jolly, balding fellow with a great bushy mustache. I instantly liked him. His laboratory, in a tiny room on the first floor, was filled with specimens and books. The news of an interesting case traveled fast, and soon, the room was crowded with students and physicians.

Professor Fitz pulled his mustache. "Won't do. Won't do. Much too crowded. We shall use the Bigelow auditorium."

We marched to a glum, ill-lit auditorium that had creaky wooden floors and the overwhelming stench of dead bodies. Students and observers lined the tier of benches that overlooked Julie's body reposing on a plain, wooden table. Even in death, Julie was still exquisite. I wiped away a tear and struggled to keep calm. Dr. Bell and I squeezed in between students on the lower bench nearest the body.

At that moment, a diminutive, frail man wearing a large bow tie and a grey, frock coat entered the auditorium. The students stomped their feet. "Hurray for Dr. Holmes!" they cheered.

The little fellow spoke with a wheezy voice. "Now, Reginald, be gracious to our guests. After all, they are from Edinburgh," he said.

The new arrival was none other than Oliver Wendell Holmes, the 'Autocrat of the Breakfast Table' and America's greatest poet. There was a brief, polite exchange concerning who should perform the autopsy, Dr. Bell or Dr. Fitz. The corpse, after all, was English. Graciously, Dr. Bell said that Dr. Fitz should have the honor of opening the body.

"Arthur, explain what happened to Julie," said Dr. Bell.

The students became very quiet when I described the events; the historic operation of separating the twins, Julie's apparent suffocation, and her ultimate and untimely death. I also exhibited the photograph of the hand print on her face.

From his first, careful midline incision in the abdomen, Dr. Fitz worked with Germanic precision to dissect the organs. "Gentlemen, observe the liver that was shared by the twins."

The students became more attentive, and Dr. Holmes stood on tiptoe to peer into the abdomen. "A miracle of surgery," he said.

Dr. Fitz dissected, organ by organ, and demonstrated that the lung floated in a basin of water. "This young lady did not die by drowning. She was definitely dead before entering the ocean," he said.

When we followed the students out of the auditorium, Dr. Holmes, with a twinkle in his eyes, grasped Dr. Bell. "By all means, stay at the Parker House and join our literary group on Saturday afternoon. The food is the best in Boston. Try the clam chowder and don't miss the Boston cream pie," he said.

"Arthur, we have the proof. Now we must convince that oaf, Baron Runcie, that the Russian count, Borovsky, is a killer," said Dr. Bell.

6 June 1883, Boston

The five-storied Parker House hotel at the foot of Beacon Hill has high, arched windows, marble steps, thick carpets, and comfortable beds. A pleasant surprise in this uncouth country. Worn out by the yesterday's activities, I slept like a dead man and awoke today to leaden skies and driving rain splattering against the windows.

Dr. Bell, still in his dressing gown, bounded to his feet, full of vigor, lit up his favorite pipe, and blew a cloud of fragrant smoke. "Arthur, Runcie has not contacted London. The confounded man is besotted with Borovsky's title. Typical. The British upper class will believe a nobleman instead of a commoner. He may very well allow Borovsky to go free without more evidence."

"Sir, what about the stones we took from his case?" I asked.

"Yes, they may be significant, but we are likely to require the assistance of a geologist if we are to learn more."

I gave the orange-colored stone to Dr. Bell, who examined it with a magnifying glass by the window. "Hmm, yellow flecks embedded in stone. Merely fool's gold, iron pyrites, or the real thing?" He paced the floor, turning the stone over and over in his hand while puffing his pipe. "Arthur, after you get something to eat, dash out to the nearest chemist and purchase one ounce of nitric acid and three of hydrochloric acid. And, yes, a small quantity of liquid mercury and a small glass flask," said he.

I paused long enough to have a capital breakfast of eggs, bacon, and a dish recommended by the waiter, Boston baked beans. After a second pot of tea, I had strength sufficient to face the rainy day. The chemist's shop was on a delightful cobbled street with posters advertising potions for every conceivable ache and pain. There was medicine for the liver and kidneys. Most, such as 'Lydia Pinkham's Vegetable Compound,' were for female ailments. They all contained a considerable amount of alcohol or opium.

The chemist raised an eyebrow at my request, but measured the acid into bottles. "Be careful. Either will eat through solid iron." He also had liquid mercury for barometers. I also purchased a small glass flask and a sack of licorice candy.

When I returned to Parker House, Dr. Bell chipped a yellow speck from the crystal and placed it in a porcelain dish filled with nitric acid. The intact speck gleamed like a gem at the bottom of the liquid. It was unaffected by the acid. Next, he added the hydrochloric acid. When the two liquids mixed, we watched as the yellow speck dissolved. "Ah, the mixture is *aquia regia*, also known as the 'acid test.' Now, one more test." He chipped off another yellow speck and placed it in the liquid mercury. The speck promptly disappeared. "This rock contains gold. Where is it from? Why did Borovsky have it?" asked Dr. Bell.

"Yes, and why did the American, Jack Dawson, carry away the sample case with Penelope? What else might be in there?" I asked.

"The best minds in Boston will be at the literary club this afternoon. Surely someone will know of a geologist," I said.

Boston is called the Athens of America for good reason. The Saturday Afternoon Literary Club met in a fine room on the second floor of the hotel. There were many notables. James Russell Lowell and John Greenleaf Whittier each read a bit of poetry. The highlight was Oliver Wendell Holmes. He stood before a cheery fire, as tall as his slight frame allowed, and read from one of his most famous poems, "The Chambered Nautilus."

Build thee more stately mansions, O my soul,
As the swift seasons roll!
Leave thy low-vaulted past!
Let each new temple, nobler than the last,
Shut thee from heaven with a dome more vast,
Till thou at length art free
Leaving thine outgrown shell by life's unresting sea!

There were huzzahs and applause when he finished. Dr. Holmes immediately made for Dr. Bell. "I knew nothing of the germ theory or of antisepsis, but I recommended cleanliness for childbirth many years ago. The profession laughed when I suggested that fevers of childbirth were carried on the hands of physicians," said Dr. Holmes.

"Pasteur and Lister have proved that you were absolutely correct. Can you recommend someone on the Harvard faculty who is a geologist?" asked Dr. Bell.

"Indeed. Alexander Agassiz is just the fellow. He is a geologist, as well as a miner and a zoologist. You can find him in the Peabody Museum," said Holmes.

Later, we tucked into green turtle soup, oysters on the half shell, venison chops, and delicious Parker House rolls.

8 June 1883

Yesterday, Bell was immersed in newspapers and books. With nothing else to do, I chose to stroll about Boston. Bostonians are a sober bunch, and the streets were crowded with black-clad people on their way to church.

Today, physicians and surgeons occupied the lower benches in the Bigelow auditorium for the first of Dr. Bell's demonstrations and lectures. The medical students in the upper tiers were more gentlemanly than the ruffians we had encountered at the Rush Medical School in Chicago five years ago. Dr. Bell lectured on Lister's antiseptic techniques in great detail using innumerable case histories of compound fractures of bones and joints infected with tuberculosis. In America, the surgeons still amputate limbs for these diseases, but Dr. Bell showed how patients could be healed while saving the limb.

Professor Bowditch, wearing a black, frock coat and a purple, satin vest, theatrically gazed about the room. "I have looked everywhere and have never seen a germ." The students roared with raucous laughter. "Now, Mr. Shattuck will present a patient to our distinguished guest," said Bowditch. I felt sorry for poor Shattuck the student who fumbled with a notebook.

The patient was about forty years old, pale, and a bit yellow, with hollow cheeks and a rather stumbling gait. His face contorted into a painful grimace each time he placed his right foot on the floor. He had a particularly severe spasm of pain when Mr. Shattuck assisted him onto the padded table.

"Reverend Ebenezer Hale has had fevers, been sick to his stomach and, during the past month, has had severe pains in his right leg," The student said.

Professor Bowditch stood, twirled his watch chain, cleared his throat, and spoke. "My diagnosis is malaria. However, there has been little response to Cinchona," he said.

I tingled with anticipation. Dr. Bell observed the patient and the poor student through half-lidded eyes. "Mr. Shattuck, our students in Edinburgh examine patients. I presume you performed the usual observations, palpation, and auscultation. What did you find in the Reverend Hale?"

"Ah, sir, we students are not allowed to examine patients," said the quivering Shattuck. Dr. Bell fixed his gaze on the patient. His restless eyes roved back and forth from face to hands and settled for a moment on Mr. Hale's coat. He counted the pulse for a full minute and then pulled down Mr. Hale's lower eyelid. He stood away from the table. "Mr. Hale, how long were you stationed in West Africa?"

"I was in Mali four years before I became too ill to preach the Gospel," Mr. Hale said.

Professor Bowditch came to his feet. "How the deuce did you know he had been in Africa?" he asked.

"A religious tract with a portrait of an African is protruding from his coat pocket. He does suffer from malaria." Dr. Bell dramatically paused, while Bowditch turned bright red. "He also has a second disease that is most commonly found in West Africa. Mr. Shattuck, please roll up Mr. Hale's right pant leg. Gentlemen, you are about to see a blister. A blister typical for Dracunculiasis." The students and physicians gasped in astonishment when Mr. Shattuck revealed a blister nearly a half-inch in diameter on the lateral side of Mr. Hale's leg. "Bah! Means nothing. It is a mere skin irritation," Dr. Bowditch exclaimed.

"Arthur, prepare a small bistoury and a toothed forceps," said Dr. Bell. I found the instruments in his case, prepared the carbolic acid, and soaked the instruments. "Now, if you please, administer a light anaesthetic to our patient." Mr. Shattuck volunteered.

When the Reverend was peacefully asleep, Dr. Bell removed his coat, rolled up his sleeves, and dipped his hands in carbolic. I swabbed the leg with the antiseptic. It was a perfect demonstration of Dr. Bell's method of preventing infections in wounds. He took up the bistoury, opened the blister, and made an incision that extended three inches up the leg. "Gentlemen, you are about to see a Guinea worm, also known as the fiery serpent because of the intense pain." He grasped a white, worm-like object that was about an eighth of one inch in diameter and gently pulled it from the wound. He paused after he had delivered perhaps six inches. "The female Guinea worm can be up to three feet long. One must remove them slowly and avoid breaking the worm. If a portion is left in the patient, the worm will die and cause a fatal infection."

It took well over an hour of patient traction to deliver the entire worm. The audience remained in their seats, speechless, as if mesmerized by the performance. The Brahmin feathers were severely ruffled by Dr. Bell's acute diagnosis.

After lunch, we took a brisk walk to the consulate. An undersecretary ushered us to Baron Runcie's office. The fellow was still in a soiled dressing gown and smacking his blubbery lips over a tumbler of gin and tonic. "Only thing for one's health," said he.

"Have you had instructions from Colonel Beach-Edwards concerning Count Borovsky?" asked Dr. Bell.

"Damn it all. Can't bother the home office with trifles. Enough trouble with these Americans. Now, the count — a fine fellow, a real sportsman. He has shot polar bears and tigers. Couldn't ask for a better man," said Runcie.

"Please, the man murdered an English woman. You must consult the Secret Service," said Bell.

Runcie waved a chubby hand. "Stuff and nonsense. Besides, an American — damn me, his name, his name is Stanford, a rich railroad man — wired the American Secretary of State to intervene and insists we set the man free."

"You must not do that without permission from the home office," said Bell.

"Yes, must not let the Americans interfere," said Runcie.

We left it at that and took our leave. I felt let down and disappointed about Her Majesty's servants, but then, I was only a lowly doctor.

9 June 1883

Immediately after a hearty breakfast, we set off to see specimens of appendicitis at the laboratory of Professor Fitz. It is an amazing collection of appendices pickled in alcohol. "These specimens came from autopsies of patients who had died with abdominal pain. I cannot convince our surgeons to operate," Dr. Fitz said.

We examined appendices with perforation. Others were gangrenous. "Clearly, an operation to remove these might be curative. It only requires the antiseptic technique," said Dr. Bell.

Dr. Bell waved me away. "Arthur, I intend to study these specimens the rest of the day. You are on your own." He was scheduled to attend a medical faculty dinner at the Harvard Club that evening. It was time for me to do a bit of sleuthing, bring Borovsky to justice, and get to the bottom of why he had murdered Julie.

I set off to find Professor Agassiz at the Peabody Museum of Archaeology and Ethnology at Harvard University in hopes of learning the origin of the rocks we had taken from Borovsky's room. I entered the two-story, red brick building and was immediately confronted with fearsome skeletons of long extinct animals, a huge turtle shell, and a Dodo. I wandered about and at last found a droopy, ancient curator who informed me that Professor Agassiz was away in Peru seeking a copper mine. "Is another geologist available?" I asked. The old fellow rustled the pages of a day book while I shifted from one foot to another.

"Ah, you are in luck. His assistant, Mr. Manfredi, is out for the day, but will return this evening. I shall put you down for an appointment. Would nine o'clock be convenient?" he asked.

"It will do."

Next, I stopped in at the consulate. Baron Runcie was unavailable. The officious clerks didn't say if he was out for a long lunch or an early tea. By great good fortune, I happened on the communications officer, a nice young man named Codlington. "Have you by any chance sent a cable concerning this Borovsky

77

fellow to Sir Cameron Beachy-Edwards in the home office?" I asked.

"No, no, nothing like that at all. The baron treats Borovsky like visiting royalty," he said. I invited Codlington out for a spot of supper and a drink. He turned out to be a jolly fellow and knew all about the new telephone system and the miraculous trans-Atlantic cable.

"Would you mind sending a personal message to Sir Beachy-Edwards?" I asked. "Glad to," said he.

I rapidly wrote a few lines on a sheet of note paper. *Dear Uncle Peachy, J.P. dead. B. suspects Nikolai Borovsky. Arthur*

We strolled back to his office in the consulate. "Some of us have rounded up a few girls for a party. Are you free later tonight?" Codlington asked.

"No, I have an appointment with a geologist at the museum." Was it my imagination? There had been a slight rustle at the door and a soft tread in the hall outside of the office. I dismissed my unease and took my leave of Codlington.

I had developed a limp and a swollen right ankle, due to an old rugby injury, so I first went to our room to fetch my walking stick before proceeding to the museum. The geological section was rather isolated in the southwest corner. After losing my way in darkened corridors and rooms filled with skeletons, I found Mr. Manfredi at a large desk facing a wall, in a large room lined with cases containing rocks, various types of earth, sand, and specimens of minerals.

"I am Arthur Conan Doyle. Thank you for seeing me."

"I have not yet had supper and am about to leave for the day, so you will need to be quick," Manfredi replied.

I produced the two rocks we'd taken from Borovsky's room. "Please, before you go, can you tell me anything about these specimens?" I asked.

He pulled an oil lamp closer and withdrew a large magnifying glass from a drawer. He scrutinized the specimen that I handed to him. "Quartzite, with a rich vein of gold," he said. He turned the second specimen over in his hands. "Ah, this is much more interesting. See these orange crystals?"

"Yes, are they of any importance?" I asked.

"It is wulfenite, also known as lead molybdate, a rich source for molybdena," said he.

"What is molybdena and the origin of the specimen?"

His eyes and hand went to a bookcase over the desk. He seemed to be pointing at a small, brown, cloth-covered book when, at the same instant, a shot rang out. The left side of Manfredi's skull exploded. Bits of shattered skull, blood, and brain splashed on my coat. I turned just in time to see a dark figure in a cloud of acrid gun smoke. He was less than twenty feet away and taking aim again. The second shot came less than a second later. The bullet tore at my sleeve, but I suffered no injury. I recalled Colonel Beachy-Edward's explaining how to use the cane as a gun. I dropped to one knee, raised my walking stick, and pressed the trigger. There was a surprised yelp, and the assailant dashed away down a darkened corridor. I could do nothing for Manfredi and gave pursuit. It was useless. The killer got away through an open window. I returned to the room where the remains of Manfredi's lifeless body still lay. I glanced up at the bookshelf and retrieved the small volume he had pointed out. The title was, *Exploration of the Yukon Territories and Alaska, 1878-80*, by Nelson Miles, General, U.S.A.

I was still hunched next to the dead Manfredi, and had only turned the first page, when there was a cry of alarm. A guard arrived and flooded the room with light from a bulls-eye lantern. I had the presence of mind to shove the volume into an inside coat pocket just before a beefy, red-faced policeman rushed into the room. He crashed his nightstick down on the back of my head. It was at least half an hour before I came to my senses, lying in a sticky pool of blood on the floor. For a long while, I saw two faces, then they merged into one. It was Detective Kennedy who had met us at the dock on our arrival.

"You are in a bit of trouble, Mr. Conan Doyle," said he. I struggled to a sitting position and, still inarticulate, pointed towards the back of the room. "Sho — shots from there," I said.

Kennedy paced the length of the room then returned. "Explain yourself."

I rose, unsteadily, to my feet and attempted to explain what happened. "There, in the wall ..." I pointed to the two holes.

Kennedy went to work with a pocket knife and soon extracted two large bullets. The detective weighed one in each hand. "At least two hundred grains, .44 calibre," he muttered. Without another word, he inspected my .32 calibre cane.

"You fired this weapon?"

"Yes, I may have winged the assailant. He escaped down the corridor and out the window."

Kennedy was still not satisfied with my explanation. My mind did not clear sufficiently to give a detailed account of my actions until we arrived at police headquarters. I was still bleary-eyed when word came to the police headquarters of a murder at the British Consulate.

"Come, Mr. Conan Doyle. You may be of assistance," said Kennedy. He beckoned me to join him in a two-horse cab. The consulate was in an uproar. The baron, still in his dressing gown, could hardly speak. My newest friend, Codlington, was dead. His head was down. One arm was stretched out over his desk. His dead hand clutched my scribbled message. The handle of a dagger protruded from his back. This was too much. I was surrounded by death. Was I responsible for this latest murder? I felt like weeping, but struggled for control.

"Mr. Kennedy, I suggest you call in Dr. Bell." I felt a wave of nausea and couldn't help getting sick on the floor.

Dr. Bell arrived within the hour. He was clean-shaven, dressed in a hound's tooth jacket, grey trousers, and freshly shined shoes. His cravat was tied perfectly. Without a word, he surveyed the communications room and stooped to inspect a crust of dirt on the floor. He rose, tore a page from his notebook, scooped the bit of dirt onto the page, and folded it carefully. He then moved to the body and gently touched a spot of blood on poor Codlington's jacket.

"The blood clot is almost dry. The wound was inflicted within the past three hours. Please, bring a lamp." Dr. Bell then stooped, minutely inspected the handle of the dagger, and circled around to the desk, where another pool of dried blood had seeped out of the victim's mouth. "A long blade. First, the lung. Then, it penetrated either the aorta or the left ventricle. Death was instantaneous. He may have recognized his assailant." Bell stood quite still for several minutes, surveying the room with his quick, grey eyes.

He nodded to Detective Kennedy. "Remove the dagger." The blood-stained dagger came out of the body easily. The blade was at least eight inches long and was sharp on both sides. "This is a type of dagger used by Cossacks," said Bell.

"Then it is of Russian origin. Where is Borovsky?" I shouted.

There was a dead silence until Baron Runcie coughed and cleared his throat. "He did not come for morning tea."

A search of the consulate revealed no trace of the Russian.

"Could he have been at the museum? Dr. Bell should investigate the crime scene at the museum," I said. Kennedy readily agreed and off we went, back to the Peabody Museum on the Harvard campus.

Dr. Bell lingered to admire the many specimens, especially the Dodo skeleton, until, with a sigh, he entered the geology section. There were still fragments of Manfredi's skull, a splash of blood, and bits of soft brain tissue on the desk. The mind sometimes turns to seemingly irrelevant items in emergency situations, and I wondered for a moment why the brain is called 'grey matter,' since fresh brain tissue is pink and covered with bluish veins.

"I fired a shot at the assailant. He was there." I pointed to the end of the room, just at the entrance to a corridor. Bell wandered about, apparently looking at specimens of minerals and plain rock, before he went to the back of the room. He stood, chin in hand, and surveyed the wall and then the floor. He stooped, rose, walked a dozen steps, went down on his knees, and scooped up a bit of dirt onto a sheet of paper.

At the desk, he beckoned to the mystified detective Kennedy and displayed the two sheets of paper with a few crusts of grey-black soil. "These are identical specimens of loamy, alluvial soil. The caking suggests they were embedded on the cleat of a boot. One man committed both murders," Dr. Bell said.

"Hah! Your companion, Mr. Conan-Doyle, admitted to being at the consulate and was here at the time of Manfredi's murder," said detective Kennedy. He was right! Would I spend months in a Boston jail attempting to clear my name? I had been falsely accused of crimes during our last trip to America, when I saved the president from assassination. The police, instead, accused me of attempting assassination. *Why did I ever think it would be worthwhile to venture again to this godforsaken country?* I thought.

"Please remove your shoes, lad," said Dr. Bell. I removed my rough brogans. The soles were worn and smooth. There was no trace of earth. "Now, come along," said Bell. He beckoned to Detective Kennedy. The good doctor easily climbed out the window used by the escaping murderer. There on the moist ground were deep prints of a cleated boot. The footprints went off to the northeast in ever-lengthening strides. "The man you seek is wearing heavy boots. Now that he has killed an American citizen, I hope that the Boston police will finally take an interest in Count Nikolai Borovsky," said Bell.

We returned to the Parker House, where, despite a throbbing head and still-sore leg, I have written down these notes and am now exhausted and ready for sleep.

10 June 1883

Today, I awoke, yawned, and rubbed the sleep out of my eyes. I was sore all over, but no worse than after a game of rugby. Dr. Bell, fully dressed and bright of eye, thrust a mug of hot, bitter coffee into my hands. "You need this. We must hurry. Our train departs before noon." I drank the bitter brew and finished off the buttered toast and a slice of cold ham that remained from Dr. Bell's breakfast.

Bell thrust a cable-gram in my hands. "I threatened to report that damn Runcie as an incompetent fool unless he sent a cable to Beachy-Edwards. I have spent the past hour deciphering his response. This is the result." *Regret death of Julie. Nikolai Borovsky, Russian, brilliant scientist, known assassin, assumes many disguises, very dangerous. Has contacts with Americans and Russians on west coast. Will send Mr. Sherlock Holmes to meet you in San Francisco. Peachy*

"Well, well, very good! Laddy, We are over our heads in this case. The Russian could put a bullet in our brain. I am happy to have Mr. Holmes take over the case," Dr. Bell said.

"But, sir, I have a personal interest in bringing the culprit to justice," I said.

The bullet had torn away a portion of the sleeve, ruining my tweed jacket. I was about to dispose of it when I remembered the moment just before Manfredi died. I thrust my hand into the inner pocket and found the small book by an American general. The two rock specimens and a balled up bit of paper fell out as well. I packed the lot into my bag.

We hurried away to the Boston, Albany and Chicago rail station, found our car, and had just enough time to settle into our compartment when the whistle blew and off we went. Our car became incredibly hot and stuffy as the train wound up and down hills, past fields and the picturesque villages of New England. In the evening, just before going to bed, I rediscovered the small, brown book by the American general. I became wide awake when, on the title page, I saw the name Nikolai Borovsky listed as both a member of the expedition and its geological consultant. The book described a survey of the mountains and rivers of Alaska and the Yukon Territory of Canada. There was no agreement as to the location of the border between the two. There was a hint, even a statement, that Russian-Alaska had included a good deal more territory than appeared on maps. The book suggested that the United States had purchased all of the Yukon and British Columbia. The only passing reference to geology was a short note about the latitude and longitude of a hill named 'King Solomon's Dome.' I sighed at this new mystery and went off to sleep.

11 June 1883, Chicago

Upon our arrival in Chicago, Angus Duncan, Dr. Bell's old university chum, met us in his splendid carriage driven by a jolly Scotsman dressed in a black top hat and all the finery of a London footman. Angus, a railway magnate, had generously hosted our previous trip to the states. When we arrived at his home, I left Mr. Duncan and Dr. Bell in the lavish drawing room, refreshing themselves with tots of single malt whisky. I immediately went to the kitchen and embraced Mrs. O'Flynn, the cook, who had become a friend during our last trip to America. I gazed into her wrinkled, motherly face, thought of my mam, and had a momentary pang of regret that I was not home looking after my family. She bustled about the kitchen and, in no time, fixed an enormous roast beef sandwich with mustard and a tankard of cold beer.

I munched on the pleasant repast and listened to her prattling. "Well, lad, now ye are a regular doctor ye can prescribe for me knees." She shyly hoisted her apron and black, wool skirt. Her knees were knobby with bony lumps from scrubbing floors on her hands and knees.

I remembered Dr. Brown's prescription for Mrs. Samuel Clemens. "I will get Arnica ointment from the chemist. It is the latest thing for rheumatism," I said.

An hour or so later, I unpacked my bag and again found the two rocks I had taken from Borovsky. While admiring the orange crystal, I replayed in my mind the assailant's booming shot and Manfredi's head exploding and leaving shards of skull and brain scattered over the desk and floor. He had just said something important about the orange crystal. In a flash, I remembered; molybdena. Manfredi had pointed to the brown book. I searched its pages, but found no reference to molybdena. I went back to the bits of rock, one with gold and the other supposedly containing the strange element. *Exploration of the Yukon Territories and Alaska* described mountain peaks, rivers, and other landmarks. There were occasional numbers indicating latitude and longitude, but none matched the numbers on my slip of paper.

Mr. Duncan, with his usual magnanimity, put on a splendid dinner to celebrate our arrival. The guests were mostly business men, but there were professors from Rush Medical College who remembered Dr. Bell's extraordinary diagnostic skills and were eager to hear the latest medical advances from Edinburgh. Our fellow Scotsman, Alan Pinkerton, the detective, arrived late. His gait was unsteady, his face was pale, and his bushy beard was completely grey. I thought he was ill, but his eyes were as keen as ever. After drinks in the drawing room, we tucked into breast of passenger pigeon, roasted new potatoes, asparagus, and a delicious Lake Michigan trout in a tomato sauce. I couldn't wait to talk with Pinkerton and went up to him immediately after dinner.

"Have you caught the James gang?" I asked. Pinkerton scowled.

"Young fella named Bobby Ford shot him in the back a year ago. He earned a handsome reward." I thought Mr. Pinkerton would mention the bit of work I had done for him, but the mission was still a national secret. "There is a worse gang out west. Damn outlaw name of Butch Cassidy is robbing banks and trains. My men can't lay a finger on him," said Pinkerton.

The talk of outlaws brought the recent murders to mind. Pinkerton began walking away, but on impulse I clutched his arm. "Sir, have you heard of a Russian, Nikolai Borovsky?" I asked.

"Never heard of him." Mr. Pinkerton turned away and joined the group smoking cigars and drinking brandy. I followed him through clouds of smoke and listened to discussions of the decline in railroad building, mine closings, and the ongoing depression. Thousands of men are still out of work.

"Leland Stanford's got the right idea. He is building a mercenary army with out of work Irish." I could not identify the speaker but pushed through the crowd.

"And who is Leland Stanford?" I asked, recalling that was the man who had wired Baron Runcie to release Count Borovsky.

"Well, if that don't beat anything. Young fella, everyone knows Leland Stanford, one of the richest men in the world. Owns railroads, mines, companies, and most of California," said a fattish man who poked a cigar in my face.

"The man is a robber baron," said Dr. Gunn, a Rush surgeon.

"If he is so rich, why is he interested in a Russian assassin, Nikolai Borovsky?" I asked.

Alan Pinkerton came across the room to my side in an instant and whispered in my ear. "If you value your health, don't ask questions about Stanford."

I knew enough to heed Pinkerton's advice and drifted away to a group of Rush doctors who surrounded Professor Bell. "Is there an analytic chemist at Rush?" I asked.

"Well, no, but there is a new fellow, name of Lange, at the Chicago Medical School," said Dr. Gunn.

"Oliver Marcy at Northwestern in Evanston is a good all-around scientist," said Angus Duncan.

12 June 1883

I rose late, had leftovers for breakfast, and was determined to learn more about the orange crystal. I walked to South State Street, boarded a cable car, and paid my ten cents. Immediately, the driver pushed a handle that grabbed the cable and off we went at ten or even twelve miles an hour.

The Chicago Medical School appeared to be deserted, since there were no summer classes. The front door of the school was locked, but at the rear of the building, I found an open door leading to the basement. The room was ice cold. By the light of a single oil lamp I saw a half-dozen naked cadavers on tables. I shrank away from a pale fellow who stared up at the ceiling with open eyes. He looked pretty fresh. It was a storage room for bodies awaiting anatomical dissection. Out of the gloom came a beetle-browed man with a barrel chest and arms that seemed to hang down to his knees. "I am looking for Professor Lange," said I.

He said nothing but beckoned me to follow. We went up two flights of stairs, through a lecture hall, and into a laboratory which housed tables covered with retort flasks and bottles of various chemicals. Without a word, my guide motioned me into a tiny, cluttered office just off the laboratory. An elaborate diploma on the wall written in German proclaimed Johan Frederick Lange as a Doctor of Science from the University of Tübingen. A middle-aged fellow with stern, Teutonic features and short, bristly, grey hair was twirling a flask over a gas flame. There were chemical stains on his shirt.

"Professor Lange?" I asked.

"Yes."

"I am Arthur Conan Doyle, of the University of Edinburgh. I have a question for you."

"Only one? Most people have dozens." He spoke with a strong German accent, but I was encouraged by his pleasant response. I placed the piece of orange crystal on his desk.

"Can you identify this specimen?" I asked.

His eyes widened and he half rose from his chair. "Where did you find this?" he asked. His hand clenched my bit of rock. His entire demeanor changed in an instant. He could barely control his voice. "It is nothing, nothing at all, an insignificant piece of quartz . . . I mean, it looks like it is nothing, may not be significant, but if you want to know for sure, why don't you leave it with me for analysis? Yes, that is it. Leave it here as I will need to analyze it just to be sure of what it is, and of course, I will let you know my findings, though I am sure it is nothing," said he, almost as if I wasn't even there and he was talking to himself.

"No, thank you. I haven't the time. Give it to me," said I, suspecting there was more to his interest in the specimen than he was stating.

He crouched like a cat, and with a cunning look, he moved to drop the crystal into a drawer. I grasped his arm with all my strength, but he still held the specimen in a death grip. "If it is of so little importance, then why don't you give it back?" I asked.

"It may have some value. I will trade a much more beautiful specimen if you are a collector."

"I am not interested," I replied, sure by this time that he was hiding some information about the crystal.

Lange turned to the beetle-browed fellow who was still at the door and nodded. The man's long arms, moving like a professional fighter's, grabbed my neck with a vicious choke hold. I couldn't breathe and would have collapsed if he had not let up the pressure. "Now, Dr. Doyle, I am serious. You must leave this specimen and inform me of its origin. You are trespassing in my laboratory. For all I know you are a common thief. My friend, Gunter, has room for you with the other thieves and derelicts in our basement cooling room."

He was right. No one would recognize another corpse awaiting anatomical dissection. I tensed the muscles in my neck and raised my shoulders a fraction of an inch. It was enough to loosen his grip. I managed to take in enough air to clear my mind and kicked back with the heel of my shoe against Gunter's knee. He grunted and loosened his grip just a fraction. I landed another kick on his knee. He let out a *whoof* of pain and wilted just enough for me to reach down and grasp my ankle stiletto. I turned the blade outward and brought the point along his leg to the groin and then to his mid abdomen. It cut through his clothing but could not have penetrated his skin more than a fraction of an inch. His surprise and pain gave me the advantage. In a moment, I had the knife at Dr. Lange's throat. "Give the crystal to me. I will leave and say nothing about this encounter." He released the orange crystal.

"Now the key to this room." His eyes bulged. I dug the point of the stiletto deeper into his skin until he reached into his pocket and produced a brass key. I closed and locked the door as fast as I was able and made a run for it.

I kept up a fast pace on Prairie Avenue, past fashionable mansions, until I was certain there were no followers. My heart raced, but instead of panicking, I grew even more determined to get to the bottom of this mystery. Mr. Duncan had mentioned a Professor Marcy, so I went into the business center and asked directions to the Northwestern University. The policeman directed me to the Chicago, Milwaukee, and Northwestern station. "Get off in Evanston, walk east to the lake. Can't miss it," he said.

University Hall was a gothic building with a grand tower set in a grove of trees overlooking the wide expanse of Lake Michigan. It was a lovely setting for a university, but not as imposing as the University of Edinburgh. A young assistant led me up flights of stairs to the Natural History Museum on the top floor of the building. There were skeletons of a whale and an elephant at one end of the room. Display cases along the wall held specimens of animals, minerals, and fossils from all over the world. Professor Oliver Marcy was at a long table surrounded by fossils. He was about sixty years old and dressed in a black frock coat. Pince-nez glasses were perched on the bridge of his nose. If nothing else, he looked like a real professor, a description I hoped was accurate given my experience with the sinister Professor Lange.

He was tracing the outline of a fossil fish on drawing paper and did not look up.

"Sir, I am Arthur Conan Doyle of the University of Edinburgh. Can you spare a moment?" I asked. He removed the glasses and squinted my way.

"Edinburgh? Do you know of John Hutton?" he asked.

"He was before my time, sir, but I know of his work with fossils. He proved the world is millions of years old."

"Ah, splendid. Quite right. How may I help you?"

"Can you identify this specimen?" I asked, not wanting to waste a moment. I placed the orange crystal on the table.

The professor adjusted his spectacles and weighed the rock in one hand. "It is lead oxidate molybdenum and very rare. So far as I know the only source is a small mine in Sweden." He patiently and methodically viewed the specimen, rolling it in his hand and looking at it from all angles.

"Is it important?" I asked.

"Young man, molybdenum is almost priceless. When mixed with iron, it produces a steel alloy of incredible strength that resists high temperatures. The world's industries, especially the munitions makers, would pay millions of dollars for a reliable source of molybdenum."

"But, sir, are there other, more readily available, alloys?" I asked.

Professor Marcy took a long look out the window at the tranquil blue surface of Lake Michigan. "With sufficient molybdenum, any munitions maker, such as the Krupps in Germany, could manufacture a cannon so strong and so light that it could be transported by a team of horses and fire a half-ton missile across the English Channel. It would also be possible to build light, powerful, steam engines that would increase the speed and safety of railroad engines."

I suddenly felt overwhelmed by fatigue, slumped in a chair, and sighed. "Do you mind telling where you obtained the specimen?" he asked.

I glanced about the room. The wooden floor creaked when I moved in my chair. Dust motes danced in sun beams shining through west facing windows. The door to the corridor was closed; we were alone. I moved closer to the professor, deciding that he was trustworthy and knowing I would need to find out more if I was to help bring Borovsky to justice.

"I am not certain, but I believe this sample came from an expedition to Alaska." I unfolded the crumpled paper with the numbers, 62:48 132:12 and placed it on the table. Without a word, he leaped to his feet, went to a shelf, and returned to spread a large map of North America on the table. He used a pair of dividers and a protractor to measure from the lines of latitude and longitude on the map. After a moment, he drew an X.

"This point is not in Alaska but in the Yukon, a part of Northern Canada. It is surrounded by high, cold mountains, rivers, and impenetrable forests. For most of the year, the land is covered with ice and snow. It is one of the most inaccessible places on earth."

"If it is so rare and can only be found in such a remote area, making it nearly unobtainable, then why is this specimen so important?" I asked.

The professor had a faraway look in his eyes, removed his spectacles, and tapped them gently on the table before he spoke. "The fact that molybdenum is rare and nearly inaccessible means that whoever gets his hands on it will attain great wealth and power. Some men — greedy, ruthless men — will do anything, go anywhere on earth, to find what they believe will enable them to acquire such dominance," he said.

I pondered this new information. "But sir, would it not take the power of a government with a great army of men to mine and transport the mineral?"

"No lad, a ruthless man could build a transport system with imported labor, just as a few men managed to build our railroads," the professor answered.

When I rose to leave, he offered a word of caution. "Forget you ever found this. Stick with medicine, young man."

After I left the professor's, my head was swirling with more questions than answers. I decided it would be wise to go back to Angus Duncan's, eat a good meal, contemplate and share my discoveries with Dr. Bell. Sure enough, a huge slab of rare beefsteak and a glass of port, delivered with a warm smile by Mrs. O'Flynn, restored my sense of well-being. After dinner, over cigars and brandy, I relayed the story of my day to Dr. Bell and Angus Duncan.

"I know of Professor Lange. Since he is not a physician, the Chicago Medical School pays him very little. He acted out of greed. The police would pay little attention to your story. Forget that episode," said Angus Duncan.

"Let me see the book about the Yukon and Alaska," said Dr. Bell. perused its pages. "Arthur, how often have I told you to pay attention to details? Look here, on the title page. Did you see this? You did not mention it. Nikolai Borovsky was not only a member of the expedition, but also a consultant to the Alaska Mill and Mining Company. That must be American." said Dr. Bell.

Despite my now being a doctor, I felt the same sense of inadequacy that I had often experienced while I was Bell's clerk so many years ago. The information was in fine print, but why had I not noticed it before?

"Sir, in the day's chaos, I merely skimmed through the book." I hoped that would serve as a reasonable excuse for missing such an important detail.

"Oh, yes, lad. To be sure," he responded, almost absentmindedly, while keeping his eyes focused on the book. "Aha, look … page forty-five, at the far eastern edge of the map here, written in small numbers, 62:48 132:12, marking a small peak, Catherine's Dome."

"Ah, that is the same latitude and longitude on the specimen" I said. Mr. Duncan put down his glass and examined the page over Dr. Bell's shoulder.

"Catherine became empress of Russia in 1773. The location of the dome on this map that is named for her suggests the Russians explored Western Canada. When Russia sold Alaska to the United States in 1867, the eastern border was in dispute. The United States could claim a good bit of Western Canada," said Duncan.

"In that case, the United States would have the molybdenum," I said.

Angus Duncan, the wily Scot, paused to re-light his cigar.

"It is more likely that Russia would claim the area beyond the boundary and even attempt to buy back all of Alaska in order to have sole access to the untapped resources like molybdena. America is in a depression, so the country needs money. The new president, 'Elegant Arthur,' must support his grand lifestyle," said Duncan.

"But wouldn't the United States back England's claim to the area?" asked Dr. Bell.

"The Americans still hate the British because of the *Alabama* affair," Duncan replied.

"What is that?" I asked.

"The British built the *Alabama* for the Confederates. She was a heavily armed cruiser that sunk sixty-five Union merchant ships. The United States is still demanding reparations."

"What does Nikolai Borovsky have to do with this?" I asked.

"He is very likely out of favor with the Russian government and is attempting to sell information to the Americans. The Russians are building a trans-continental railroad that will reach the Pacific Ocean within a year. The Russians and Americans could control the entire North Pacific Ocean and, with very little force, take over Western Canada. The British are stretched thin all over the world, from India to Egypt, and the Trans-Canada Railroad is bogged down. It would be easy for the Americans to take over British Columbia," said Mr. Duncan.

Dr. Bell stretched his long legs and clasped his hands over his chest. "Borovsky is up to no good. Perhaps he hopes to gain by playing off the great powers against each other. What else is in his specimen case, and where is it now? The American and Penelope snatched the case. It is quite likely Borovsky is seeking it." said Dr. Bell.

"If that is so, Penelope may be in danger," I said.

13 June 1883

As soon as Angus Duncan let us off at the Union Station so we could get on our way to San Francisco, he hailed a uniformed Negro porter. "George, take this luggage to these gentlemen's sleeping car, number four," he said.

Our quarters were a veritable hotel on wheels. The interior was of shiny, varnished, walnut panels, and we had two berths that were, during the day, comfortable seats. George, the porter, bustled about, putting away our luggage on convenient racks, dusting the seats to remove every speck of dust. Dr. Bell gave him a five-dollar bill.

"George, how did Mr. Duncan know your name? Are you a friend of his?" asked Dr. Bell. The porter flashed a mouthful of white teeth.

"No suh. My name is Willy, but all us porters are called 'George' after Mr. George Pullman who makes these here fine sleeping cars."

Within an hour, we had left Chicago and were speeding across western Illinois past small farms, fields of knee-high corn, cows, and pigs. It seemed like every farmer out tending his fields waved at the train. I always waved back. Along towards dusk, we crossed a fine, new bridge over the Mississippi River at Davenport and were in Iowa. After our sumptuous dinner, I listened for a while to the rhythmic *clickety-clack* of the wheels, which lulled me into a renewing sleep. I woke to the mournful sound of the train's whistle, which hooted each time we passed one of the many small towns along the way.

14 June 1883

We crossed the Missouri river at Council Bluffs, where the west really starts, but we made a dogleg to Omaha where the trains stopped long enough for us to get out and stretch our legs. There was a fine new station and a bustling town, but there was no time to explore.

I had planned to study for the doctorate examination during our trip, but I was glued to the window, just watching the plains roll by. After we passed the Mississippi bluffs, the land was flat and the sky so big you could see for miles and miles. At first, there were fields of green wheat with windmills, farm houses, and men and boys hard at work. After a while, there was just grass so high that a man on horseback could scarcely see over the top. We stopped at little towns, like Elkhorn, that weren't much more than a half-dozen saloons alongside a dusty street, a bank, a store, and, at the end of the street, maybe a courthouse. I kept on the lookout for buffalo and wild Indians, but there weren't any, not a one. After a while, the landscape changed again. Amazing! There were no trees, except a few stragglers along a creek bed, the grass grew shorter, and the land was mostly sand and dust.

Late in the day, we stopped for a whole twenty minutes at a little town, Grand Island, where a sorry band of Indians with sway-backed horses met the train. The young ones put on a little show and the passengers threw nickels and dimes to them. Dr. Bell gave them two silver dollars. There were a couple of old fellows with handsome, brown, creased faces and feathers in their hair. Because of their dress and the way they stood apart, I supposed they were chiefs. They kept off to the side and seemed to scowl at us whites. I was sorely disappointed. Where were the stalwart Redskins I had dreamed about as a boy? For a while, I had planned to write a novel about a great battle with bows and arrows pitted against rifles, but the Indians would win and capture a fair maiden. A hero, like Sir Walter Scott's Ivanhoe, would go to her rescue.

We followed the wide, muddy Platte River, and off to the north, there were rolling sand hills and a lot of dust that turned the sky grey. One time, a couple of cowboys raced alongside the train on their horses. They waved and fired pistols, but they couldn't keep up with the iron horse. The big thrill of the day was seeing a herd of antelope, leastwise that is what Willy, our porter, called them. They are fine animals — long-legged, with curling horns and a patch of white on their chest. I never saw an animal run so fast. I watched all that landscape slide by until the moon went down.

15 June 1883

It was a long way across the state of Nebraska before, in the far distance, we could see snaggle-toothed, snow-covered mountains. Folks said they were fifty miles away, but they sure looked close. The Wyoming territory had the same grass but was more barren and dry; even the people looked sort of dried out. We came to Cheyenne about the middle of the day. The two trains ahead of us were stopped on the tracks. Willy brought the bad news. A landslide had destroyed the west end of the Dale Creek Bridge and our train would be stopped for at least two weeks.

Dr. Bell hardly ever lost his composure, but he was sorely disgruntled. "I am scheduled to give lectures and a demonstration in San Francisco ten days from now."

"Mebbe you can take the Denver and Rio Grande through the mountains to Salt Lake City. It's a run-down little train that sometimes don't run on account of the owners are broke, but it's as good a chance as any fo' getting' there," said Willy. That sounded promising, but the train for Denver wouldn't leave until late in the afternoon. Our train wasn't even up to the depot, so Willy dumped our luggage out on a dusty road beside the tracks.

"You can get something to eat and rest at the Cheyenne Club" said he, pointing the way.

Every horse and wagon in town was busy hauling passengers and their baggage to rooming houses or hotels. Dr. Bell carried the instrument case, and I picked up my bag and tossed his trunk on my shoulder. It was hard going until an old fellow came by in one of those contraptions called a buckboard. It was nothing but a wooden box on four wheels hitched to a pair of horses.

"Hey, you boys need a lift?"

"Yes sir," said I. We climbed aboard.

"You kin call me Bearskin Charlie," said the driver, a runty man with tobacco-stained whiskers down to his belt. He had a double-barreled shotgun across his lap. The wagon didn't have springs or cushions and the horses mainly switched their tails against the flies, but it beat walking. We plodded for a mile or so over a street thick with horse manure and dust. Once, we had to stop for nearly a half-hour while cowboys drove a herd of cows down the middle of the street. Every man in town carried a big Colt revolver in a holster and a Winchester by his saddle.

Bearskin Charlie, spit a stream of tobacco juice and hit a fly.

"You fellows will like the club. Got the purtiest girls in the territory and any kind of gamblin' you want. Food ain't bad neither," he said.

Dr. Bell gave him a silver dollar. "Wait for us and there will be another dollar for you."

The Cheyenne Club was about the grandest building west of Chicago. The main room on the first floor had plush carpets, gas lights, and comfortable easy chairs. Two gilt staircases led to the private rooms upstairs. I guess that's where the 'purty girls' stayed. Dinner was listed for seventy-five cents. I ordered antelope steak, mashed potatoes, beans, and cherry pie with coffee. The antelope was stringy and tough as an old cow. The coffee was bitter and still had egg shells and grounds. We were about finished with the meal when a waiter came and poured a tumbler full of clear liquid for the man at the next table. The fellow took one swallow, commenced to cough, then his legs kicked out and his eyes rolled back. I went to his aid immediately, thinking he was having a fit. I clapped him on the back and his eyes opened.

"Are you alright?" I asked.

"Jest finer than a damn fiddle. That there moonshine will make a prairie dog spit at a mountain lion," said he.

After dinner, Dr. Bell retired to the reading room with his pipe and a pile of newspapers while I went upstairs to look around. There was a lot of giggling and carrying on behind closed doors, but no girls were in sight. A fellow with a big pistol on his belt looked me over outside a closed door.

"I wouldn' go in there if I was you," said he.

"Why not?" I asked.

"A poker game's been goin' on all day. Dangerous Dan McGrew is playing a woman. Don't that jes' beat all?" he answered. I went in anyway, carrying my walking stick like a fine English gentleman. The room was maybe sixty or seventy feet long and about as wide, with a long bar down one wall and a little stage.

The windows were covered with black curtains, and the room was lit with gas lights. In spite of a big crowd of tough-looking men and a few painted ladies, it was quiet as a graveyard. Over in one corner, a woman in a long, red dress was sitting alongside of an upright piano. The crowd was around a table in the middle of the room. I squeezed close enough to see a man in a black frock coat with a black hat shuffling cards. His face was like a piece of granite, and he had the meanest blue eyes I ever saw. I figured he was Dangerous Dan. The woman's back was to me, but when I pushed my way around, I saw she was Penelope, known in polite society as Lady Walshingham. I caught my breath. Her hair was done up in a bun, like a school teacher, but instead of her fancy gowns, she wore a satiny, purple shirt with long sleeves tucked into a pair of men's pants. There was a big pile of gold eagle coins, silver dollars, and greenbacks in the middle of the table. I wanted to call out to her, but out of curiosity, and with good sense, I stayed quiet and watched the play. Dangerous Dan shuffled and dealt the cards. Penelope threw down a card and picked another, then showed her hand. Penelope had three aces. She reached for the pile in the middle of the table, but Dangerous Dan pulled a two-shot derringer.

"You pulled that last ace out of your sleeve," he said. The crowd howled.

"I knowed it! I knowed for sure, that woman cheats!" one young cowboy yelled. I didn't even remember if it was loaded but I poked my walking stick against Dangerous Dan's head.

"Put down that pistol or I'll blow your head off," said I. My hand trembled worse than if I held a scalpel to a sick patient. The room went quiet. Dangerous Dan held that little pistol on Penelope and never batted an eye. Did he know I was bluffing? All of a sudden, the lady in red brought her hands down on the keys and beat out a lively tune on the piano. The whole place calmed down. She looked over her shoulder and smiled at Dangerous Dan. The scowl never left his face and his jaw clenched until I thought he would crack a tooth; after a whole minute, he nodded his head just a little and lowered the gun. I shoved the pile of money to McGrew, grabbed Penelope, and we charged out of that place like two scared rabbits.

I called to Dr. Bell when we passed the reading room and picked up our luggage.

"Do you have a bag?" I asked Penelope.

"Not a thing. Just what's on me. I'm cleaned out," she said.

I had to give Bearskin Charlie a whack to wake him up. We put Penelope on the bottom of the wagon and covered her with feed sacks.

"Head for the Denver station," said Dr. Bell.

It was a dinky little train, on account of the rails were only three feet apart and it didn't go near fast enough to suit me. I expected Dan McGrew and a band of armed men would hold up the train any minute. As soon as we settled down, Penelope spit like a cat.

"He ran away on the last train to San Francisco and left me with nothing," she said.

"Who left?" I asked.

"Why that damn Jack Dawson, that's who," said Penelope.

"What happened to the red leather case?"

"Took the case and all the money. I had to sell my clothes and jewelry to get a stake. Now it is all gone. Damn that Dan McGrew."

****

Editor's note: Arthur Conan Doyle met and indeed sought out prominent literary figures during his lifetime. This episode with Dangerous Dan McGrew may be the only time he encountered a fellow who would become a literary character rather than an author. Dangerous Dan McGrew met his death in the Malamute Saloon in the Yukon Territory during the Alaskan Gold Rush. The Lady in Red (known as 'Lou') was there, but that time, she could not protect her lover from a 'man in a buckskin shirt that was caked with dirt.' In the poem, "The Shooting of Dan McGrew," (from *Songs of a Sourdough*, Barse &Co. New York, N.Y. Newark N.J. 1916) Robert W. Service, the English Poet, described the murder scene.

"But I want to state, and my words are straight, and I'll bet my poke they're true,
That one of you is a hound of hell . . . and that one is Dan McGrew."

Then I ducked my head, and the lights went out, and two guns blazed in the dark;
And a woman screamed, and the lights went up, and two men lay stiff and stark.

Pitched on his head, and pumped full of lead, was Dangerous Dan McGrew,
While the man from the creeks lay clutched to the breast of the lady that's known as
  Lou.

16 June 1883

We arrived in Denver covered with soot, sweat, and grime. Straw and oats were stuck in Penelope's hair, and her face was streaked with dirt. Despite our meager appearance and the need to lose no time, we were happy to be in Denver, the only city with real amenities between San Francisco and Chicago. On the advice of a depot lounger, we hailed a one-horse cab and set out down the street for the Windsor Hotel. It did our hearts good to see the Union Jack flying from one turret and the flag of Windsor Castle on another. An English syndicate owned the hotel; we expected a royal welcome. The cab driver hauled our baggage to the front entrance beneath an elegant, iron porte-cochère that was flanked by two electric lampposts. Instead of a royal welcome, however, a porter in a swell gold-braided uniform and a top hat looked at our disheveled appearance and refused us entrance. He was totally without grace until Penelope turned on her upper-class English charm.

"My dear man, please announce my arrival to your manager. I am Lady Penelope Walshingham," she said in her best plummy English voice. The manager rushed out and swept Penelope right up to the lobby. We were only halfway up the front staircase when a body tumbled past our startled eyes and crashed onto the first landing. I immediately ran to the man and put my finger to his carotid artery, but he was already dead with a broken neck. Two porters removed the body with speed and nonchalance as if a dead body tumbling down a staircase was an everyday occurrence.

Dr. Bell demanded an explanation. "It is those miners. They go up to the cattlemen's room and bet all the gold they found after a year's work. When they lose, the damn fools go crazy with rotgut hooch and jump from the fifth floor to end it all," the porter explained.

Penelope bowled over the manager who, after a lot of bowing and scraping, ensconced her in a suite with a gold-plated bath tub. We took a room that cost two dollars and fifty cents. It was pure luxury, but nothing compared with the Roman bath area that was connected to the hotel through a tunnel. I hustled to the baths and sunk down in hot artesian water that bubbled up from way underground.

17 June 1883

Dr. Bell insisted we leave at the crack of dawn. The Denver, South Park and Pacific train was nothing more than a dinky steam engine, one wooden passenger car, a baggage car, two box cars, and one car for cattle. We flung Dr. Bell's trunk and my portmanteau into the baggage car and climbed aboard. Penelope sat next to Dr. Bell, since he was the best dressed and most respectable looking man on the train. I took the only seat left, next to a grizzled miner who smelled of old sweat and booze. "This shore beats packin' in grub on mules," he said. The old boy punched me in the chest and slapped his leg. "This here train goes ta durned near every town in the state of Colorado. We might even make it to Leadville, if'n we don't run off the tracks," he said.

I settled down to watch the valley of the South Platte River roll by while we chugged along a bubbly little stream. "That there is Buffalo Creek. Found a nugget there once," said my companion. Dr. Bell unfolded a week-old newspaper, *The San Francisco Morning Call*.

"Well, it says here, that Leland Stanford is donating six Gatling guns to the Bear State Militia," said he. I came out of my sleepy reverie with a jolt.

"We heard that name before," said I.

"That damn Jack Dawson said he was going to make a fortune with Stanford," said Penelope. I wondered why a millionaire was interested in the most lethal weapon known to man but let it go when I remembered that Alan Pinkerton had warned me not to mention the man's name.

We stopped at a little town named Como to fill the boiler with water and, in Garo, all the passengers went into a dirty saloon for lunch. All they had was beef stew, but the hunks of meat could just as well have been rhinoceros it was so tough. We kept going up and up and still higher as we got into the mountains. I thought we had great mountains in Scotland, but these were the highest, most rugged, and beautiful mountains in all the world. My seatmate got off at a little cluster of shacks, called Climax, and we pulled into Leadville in the late afternoon.

Leadville is a thriving little city with no less than five churches and six banks. We made for the Clarendon Hotel. Next door there was a fine brick building, the Grand Tabor Opera House. Emblazoned across the front of the building was a notice for an address on 'Art Decoration by Oscar Wilde.' I had heard the name and recalled having read one of his poems. Dr. Bell was all for meeting him since Wilde's father was a notable eye and ear surgeon.

The program started at seven o'clock in the evening; the place was packed with unruly minors and cowboys who hooted when Wilde appeared on the stage. After a coughing fit that seemed to last minutes, a tall, skinny fellow with a silver badge hollered at the men to behave themselves or he would shoot the first one who let out a squeal. The man next to me nudged my elbow. "That there is Doc Holliday. He used ta' be a darn good dentist — coulda' pulled a tooth from a wild buffalo if he had to. Then he done fell ill with the tuberculosis, came out west here, and became more of a gunslingin' gamblin' man. Folks claim he's the fastest gun in the west. Word has it he and the Earp brothers won a gunfight in Arizona. Place called the O.K. Corral. Thirty shots in thirty seconds. Fancy that! One of the bloodiest street fights in our country's history and that man you see 'afore you walked away with just a wound. The men on the other side weren't so lucky, I can tell you that. That man got more lives in him than a damn cat," he said.

Wilde had long, black hair and was pale of face. He wore a black coat, knee pants and silk stockings. He got everyone's attention from the moment he spoke the first words. "A man can be happy with a woman as long as he does not love her," he said. There were also loud guffaws when he said that we are all in the gutter. When he shared his philosophy of aestheticism, though, most of the crowd seemed to fall asleep.

Penelope, ever on the lookout for a savior, figured he was rich and was excited about meeting him. At the end of the lecture, Dr. Bell went up to the stage and invited Mr. Wilde to the bar in the hotel for a drink. Penelope gave him the eye and twitched her hips, but Wilde didn't pay her any attention. I wasn't sure if I felt bad for the poor woman or glad that she was being treated the way she had oft-times behaved towards me. We were talking about writing, poetry, and the like when he looked up at a sign above the bar, *'Don't shoot the piano player. He is doing the best he can.'* "That is the best art criticism you will ever see," Wilde said.

Though Dr. Bell went off to bed, I found Wilde easy to talk with, and pretty soon, we found a common interest in sport, especially boxing. The patrons of the Clarendon Hotel bar were a quiet bunch, but near midnight, three miners came through the swinging doors. They were all muscle and gristle and looking for trouble. Folks backed up against the walls, leaving a clear space in front of the bar.

"There's them dam furiners." The speaker swayed in his boots and pointed at us with his fist.

"That one, there, the pretty boy with hair like a girl. Fellows, let's give him a haircut," said the brutish miner. Oscar Wilde leaned with his back to the bar, propped on his elbows. I stepped aside while Penelope ducked away.

"Let's give 'em a good thrashing," said the second man. The miner who came at Wilde had an ear that looked as if it had been beaten by a hammer and a broken nose, likely from many a battle. I had a sinking feeling that we might not survive a fight. Wilde stood his ground until the big fighter came at him with flailing arms, then stepped aside and landed a solid punch on the fellow's nose. The miner backed up a couple of steps, with blood pouring down his face. He let out a tremendous roar, put down his head, and held his enormous clenched fists with arms together out in front of his body. He started out at a run, but I managed to get my foot between his ankles. He tripped forward, and Wilde landed an upper cut on his chin. I couldn't keep track of all that happened next, but there was a general melee. The three miners were throwing wild punches while Wilde and I held them off, mainly by keeping out of their way and occasionally landing a well-aimed blow. Thankfully, three deputies with tin badges came through the swinging doors. One fired a deafening pistol shot and ended the brawl. The law officers took the three bloodied miners off to spend a night in jail. When it was all over, Penelope counted a wad of greenbacks on the bar.

"I bet on you boys, had five to one odds," said she.

18 June 1883

The train for Salida, our next scheduled stop, was waiting for a shipment of silver ore. We couldn't leave until almost noon. It started out as a fine afternoon. We traveled down a valley next to the Arkansas River with mountain peaks up to fourteen thousand feet on either side.

When we pulled in to Buena Vista, a collection of shacks and saloons along one street, the train stopped and the engineer banked the boiler fire. "When do we get on to Salida?" I asked.

"Next train to Salida leaves on Monday," the conductor said.

"But we bought tickets for Salida leaving today."

"You kin sure enough use yer tickets next Monday when we got a load of cargo," he replied. We were in a fine fix. Dr. Bell was anxious to get on to San Francisco.

We were in the middle of the dusty street, with our baggage, hoping for a stagecoach, when two young fellows came busting out of a place called The Palace Manor. The boys stumbled and landed in the dirt as if they had been kicked in the backside. It was peculiar because both had on big hats, but their pants were down around their knees, as if they had left in a big hurry. A belligerent, cross–eyed woman followed the pair out the door and threw two belts with holstered pistols and two sets of leather chaps into the street.

"You good-fer-nothing, cheap, scoundrels! Next time you pay, ya' hear!" she hollered.

"Old cock-eyed Liz sure gets mean," one boy said. He looked up at Penelope and a big smile crossed his face. "Why you are the purtiest woman I ever did see."

Penelope blushed and pushed a lock of hair back from her eyes. "Why, thank you! That is the nicest thing a man ever said to me." The first fellow had a boyish grin on his handsome face. He had a square jaw and even, white teeth. Both boys had fuzz on their upper lip as if they were trying to grow a mustache. They couldn't have been more than sixteen or seventeen years old. The boys got up out of the dirt, pulled up their pants, and buckled up their belts with leather holsters that held ancient revolvers.

The first young fellow tipped his hat to Penelope, "I'm Butch. This here is Sundance. Happy to be of service," said he.

Penelope gave him a big smile that promised good things to come. "We are looking for a means of transportation to Salida," she said. "Shucks, if you don't mind ridin' horseback, we kin get you there, easy as pie," said Butch.

"How much?" asked Dr. Bell.

"Let's say ten dollars apiece, and we will go along and guide," Butch replied.

The boys took off down the street, turned a corner and, within half an hour, returned riding nice-looking horses and leading four more. "We figured you needed an extra horse to carry that there trunk and bag," said Butch. Dr. Bell gave the boys forty dollars. The two of them lashed our baggage on top of a sway-backed mare. Sundance held his hands together for Penelope to mount her horse, but instead, she leaped into the saddle as if she had been born to ride. The boys were clearly impressed. Dr. Bell did a credible job of stepping into the stirrup and swung his leg over the saddle. My horse was a big roan gelding named Tom that sidestepped and shook his head when I put a foot in the stirrup. "Scratch his ear and talk to him," said Butch. I gingerly got close enough and rubbed his forehead. Tom looked at me with huge eyes and twitched his tail. I had been on a horse twice before, during our last trip to America, and I had lost the knack of climbing aboard. Sundance had to give me an extra push before I got a leg over that big, leather saddle.

We set off on a road that was no more than a couple of dirt tracks. After we left the flat valley, the trail turned steep and rocky. Butch and Sundance seemed to be in a hurry and kept us going at a fast trot. When the horse bounced up and down, the saddle slapped my backside until I was sore and bruised. We followed a tumbling stream that was dimpled with trout coming to the surface to eat insects. I saw a little herd of deer and a huge elk higher up the mountain to our left. Butch and Sundance kept looking back over their shoulders, as if watching for followers. We kept up a fast pace. and had gone about ten miles, or maybe a little more, when I heard horses hooves. I peered back, and saw a growing cloud of dust.

Black dots came out of the dust cloud, and pretty soon, it became clear a bunch of men on horses were following us. They beat their horses and moved at a good clip.

"Oh, Oh. Time we skedaddled out of here!" Butch yelled. The two boys splashed across a creek and galloped into a patch of pine trees. Within a minute, they were out of sight. Dr. Bell, Penelope, and I looked at each other, astounded. In less than two minutes, three men with drawn pistols had us surrounded. Three others fired their guns and went off after Butch and Sundance. Their leader had a scar that went from his forehead, across an empty eye socket, and on down his cheek. He wore leather chaps, big spurs, and a battered felt hat. All three were covered with red dust, and their horses were winded.

"Damn horse thieves! We oughta string you up right now!" he yelled. His two companions uncoiled ropes from their saddles and shook out a big loop. I was too scared to talk.

Penelope blushed crimson, wiggled in her saddle, and looked at the men with puppy dog eyes.

"Gentlemen, I think there has been a misunderstanding. We did not steal anything. When our train to Salida was postponed, we rented these horses for ten dollars apiece from those two boys who rode off into the woods." The leader took off his hat, scratched his bald head, and took a long look at the three of us. Dr. Bell was wearing his deerstalker hat to keep the sun out of his eyes and a light brown suit with a cravat and waistcoat. We were dressed for train travel and had clearly never expected to go on horseback.

"Are you damn Yankees?"

"I am English and they are Scots," said Penelope. The fellow with the scarred face relaxed a bit.

Scar face waved his pistol. "Get down off my horses."

Penelope and Dr. Bell slid off their horses but I fell flat in the dust.

"Paw, kin we shoot em?" asked one of the riders.

"Don't go wastin' a bullet. It's them two boys what stole our horses. They's the ones to shoot." The youngest of the group untied our baggage and flung Dr. Bell's trunk down in the dirt. They rode

111

off, leading the horses across the creek and into the woods, leaving us in the middle of a dirt road that was hardly more than a path.

The sun had already disappeared behind the mountains and a chill wind came down the valley. Penelope's teeth were chattering and I shivered with cold. We picked up our belongings. Dr. Bell led the way to a clump of trees by the stream where we were out of the wind. He gave Penelope his heavy cloak, and I put on another jacket. It was still cold. I had the presence of mind to collect dry wood and lit a fire. We huddled together, not saying anything. Penelope went to sleep leaning against my shoulder. An animal made a mournful howl back in the woods and Penelope snuggled closer. I had dreamed about such a moment when she would lean on me for comfort. It should have been romantic, but I could not stop shivering.

19 June 1883

I dozed off until the day dawn. It was cold and grey clouds rolled down the mountain. The fire was dead. We hadn't had a single morsel to eat since leaving Leadville. My stomach growled. Dr. Bell struck a Lucifer to twigs and dry grass. He added more wood and fanned the flames until we could warm ourselves at the fire. We were about ready to set off walking along the stream when from around a corner came a barefoot boy leading a plodding, black horse. The boy wore only a leather vest and a breechclout. A leather case slung over his shoulder held a bow and a bundle of arrows.

A skinny, old man sat on the horse with dangling feet. There was no saddle or stirrups, only a wool blanket, but he sat on the horse straight as a ramrod. The old man wore leather breeches and a patched, cotton shirt. There was a leather circlet with a feather around his long hair. He also had a necklace of polished, curved teeth around his neck. The boy gave us a surprised glance, but the old man remained stiff and upright. He looked straight ahead. I limped up to the trail and held up a hand. The old fellow paid no attention, but the boy stopped and stared at me. I pointed down the trail.

"Is that the way to Salida?" I asked.

The boy pulled the rope and started the horse. "Yes."

"We are lost. Since you are an Indian you must know the way to Salida?" I said.

"I am Ta Pu Chet of the Tabaguache. The white people say we are Mountain Utes," said the boy.

"Who is he?" I asked.

"Taiwai, my grandfather, a great medicine man."

"Where are you going?" I asked. The boy pursed his lips and pointed to the highest snow covered peak.

"I am taking grandfather to the sacred mountain. The bear will tell him how to find the hole in the sky so he can see the sun and the moon and the stars. Then Grandfather will go off on his own to die," the boy said.

Dr. Bell had been watching the old man thoughtfully while smoking his great calabash pipe. Its smoke drifted over the trail.

"The old man has cataracts and is blind," said Dr. Bell. I moved closer. Sure enough, the old man's eyes were milky white and completely opaque.

Without saying a word, Dr. Bell touched the old man's hand. The man still sat straight, but opened his fingers, whereupon Dr. Bell lightly placed his great calabash pipe into the medicine man's palm. "Please accept this pipe and tobacco," he said. The old man sat still for a moment, then moved his lips, as if in prayer, while raising the pipe towards the sky. After a moment he brought the pipe to his mouth, clenched the stem between his teeth, and took in a lung full of smoke, which he slowly blew out in a great, round cloud.

"I am also a medicine man. Have your grandfather come down from the horse," said Dr. Bell. The boy spoke softly and then with both hands helped the old man slide off the horse. He could hardly stand. We helped him to sit on a rock where Dr. Bell peered into his eyes with a hand lens.

"The cataracts are mature. I can easily remove them and he will see." The boy and the old man chattered back and forth in their language.

"He says the white man's tobacco is very good. If the medicine for eyes is as strong, he will take the medicine," said the boy.

"Sir, you can't operate here," I said.

"Arthur, surgeons have operated on cataracts in the open air ever since the Hindu's invented the operation. Fetch water from the stream and make up the carbolic." I watched, fascinated, as Dr. Bell cleaned his hands and put a sharp, curved scalpel with a wooden handle, a slender forceps, and a dainty pair of iris scissors on a clean metal tray. The old man happily puffed on the calabash, even while Dr. Bell put belladonna drops in his eyes and then two percent cocaine.

"Tell him he must stay still while." Dr. Bell said. The boy spole a few words to the old man. I held the leather circlet about his head, but the boy motioned me away.

"Do not touch his head. He will remain still," said the boy. Dr. Bell sat on a rock beside his patient and, with one hand, held his lids apart. With his other hand, he made a small incision in the sclera and then inserted the small scissors into the globe of the eye. When he was satisfied, he plucked out the white lens with his forceps. Instantly, he closed the lids.

"Arthur, apply a tight bandage." He shifted position to the left eye and repeated the operation. I bandaged each eye as tightly as possible.

"He must lie absolutely still until tomorrow," Dr. Bell said. The old Indian was light as a feather when we carried him to the clump of trees by the stream and put him down on the saddle blanket.

"Sir, do you plan to stay here another day? Shouldn't we be on our way?" I asked.

"Tut, tut, my boy. We must not abandon our patient, even if we are late," said Dr. Bell.

There wasn't much to do but keep the fire going and drink water directly from the stream. After saying a few words to his grandfather, the boy set off up the mountain with his bow and arrows. He returned in late afternoon with the skinned carcass of a small deer slung over his shoulder. I never tasted anything as delicious as that venison roasted over an open fire. The boy carefully cooked slices of deer heart over the fire and fed them to the old man. That night, we slept well under the stars.

20 June 1883

We woke with the sun. When Dr. Bell removed the the old man blinked his eyes, looked into the face of the boy, and then turned his eyes to the high snow-covered peak. Dr. Bell selected a small convex lens from his case.

"Tell him to look through the glass," Dr. Bell said. The old man's dark face creased with a huge smile. He spoke rapidly to the boy.

"He says you have made great medicine. He can see an eagle flying," the boy said. It was necessary to bind the old man's eyes again, but he was clearly pleased.

We finished the last of the roast venison and helped the old man up on the horse. Then, we tied the trunk and my bag on behind and set off together down the trail to Salida. At first, it was steep and rocky, but after a few miles, we came upon a broad, flat valley with fields of barley and oats. Just at the outskirts of town, the boy stopped. "We turn here."

Dr. bell grasped the old man's hand, but spoke to the boy. "He must keep the bandages on his eyes for two weeks."

The old man untied the leather thong around his neck and gave Dr. Bell a polished tooth. "Grandfather is grateful for your medicine and wants you to have this. He says it is a tooth from a great bear. It will give you good luck," the boy said.

"You have been kind to us. May we meet again," I said.

We trudged, lugging our baggage for nearly a quarter mile until a farmer driving an empty hay wagon came by. We were all woebegone and Penelope was about done in. The farmer took pity and gave us a ride to the Monte Cristo Hotel, a fine new establishment on First Street in Salida. It was the middle of the afternoon, but we descended on the dining room like a flock of hungry wolves. The only food left was a sandwich they called the Monte Cristo, which had layers of turkey, swiss cheese, and ham, all smothered with currant jelly and fried in butter. I never tasted anything so good.

We were anxious to get on with our journey, but the next train west wouldn't leave until noon on the twenty-second. This was bad news, but there was nothing to do but lounge around the hotel and eat the local fare.

22-23 June 1883

There was no hurrying the Denver and Rio Grande Western Railroad. We crept along the sides of mountains on a track that was only three feet wide, stopped for water and coal at dinky little towns, and stayed overnight in Gunnison, a dusty mining town. Today, we went through the scariest part of the trip yet, the gorge in Black Canyon. We were surrounded by sheer rock walls which were thousands of feet high and stretched to the sky. To make matters even scarier a fierce river roared below the narrow, rickety track. Luckily, we got to Cimarron just in time to catch a train to Salt Lake City. More and more, it appears that we will be late for Dr. Bell's San Francisco lecture at four o'clock on the afternoon of the twenty-fifth of June.

24 June 1883

We had a piece of good luck today because a brand new line of the Denver and Rio Grande and Western Railroad went straight through to Ogden, Utah. We made good time over the flat, desert land and, with only one short stop, arrived in Salt Lake City. We pulled into the depot at about noon and ran to the Central Pacific ticket office.

There was a near riot as shoving men and women attempted to buy tickets, but they were turned away. My attention was drawn to a fellow wearing a black sack coat, buttoned to the neck, and stovepipe pants. He stood quietly. I would not have picked him out of the crowd until he turned his head and I saw a glint of steel in the brim of his derby hat. I became instantly suspicious, as an English thug could slice an opponent to ribbons with only his derby for a weapon. I clutched Dr. Bell.

"Hold back. That fellow looks like trouble," I said.

Dr. Bell leaned to Penelope, "Do you recognize that man?"

"No," said Penelope.

He was not a large man, but I began to imagine scenarios in which he attacked us, even though I knew I could handle him if I could dodge the slicing edge of his hat. I didn't think that Manfredi's killer would have been able to follow me, but I had still been anxious since his murder. The heavy barrel of my walking stick gun would give me an advantage if I could club him before he closed in. I had worked myself into such a frenzy that I broke into a cold sweat as we approached the ticket window.

A fat woman with a half-dozen kids knocked me out of the way with her umbrella. "We been waitin' for a train near t'all day. Don't push yourself ahead of the line." I fell back, almost into the arms of the man in the derby hat. Expecting trouble, I half-cocked my arm back to get in the first blow when he coolly held out a picture of Dr. Bell.

"Claudius Pew, at your service. I am a Pinkerton railroad detective. We've been looking for you all up and down the line."

"Are you arresting us?" I asked.

119

"No sir. I got orders to escort you on a special train all the way to San Francisco." I breathed a sigh of relief.

"Why?" Dr. Bell asked.

Mr. Pew doffed his perfectly ordinary derby hat. "They never told me, but I heard they want you for a special consultation on a sick chink. If he dies, they say the Chinamen will riot and burn the city."

With a sense of relief at having averted potential danger — and the opportunity to be escorted to the west without further trouble — we climbed into a grand sleeper coach, the only car connected to an engine that already had steam. I have never seen a train go so fast. We swayed around curves and barely slowed for hills. There was no dining car, but the conductor had a small stove to heat coffee and tea, and had laid in enough cold chicken, roast beef, bread, and butter to last the trip.

25 June 1883

We came out of the hills to Oakland and reached the Union Pacific Dock by mid-morning. The Pinkerton man whisked us onto a ferry, and we crossed the bay to the San Francisco side.

"There is no time to lose. I have telegraphed ahead for a carriage and the proper officials," Claudius Pew said. The huge bay was enveloped in a cold fog, but in clear areas we could see Chinese fishing boats, mail steamers from across the Pacific, a frigate flying the Russian flag, and a variety of smaller craft. The clocks on top of the ferry terminal chimed noon when we exited the building to a crowd of horse-drawn cabs, produce wagons, and streetcars. The delegation of city officials waiting for us was not a welcoming committee from the American Society of Surgery as I had thought. Instead, the uniformed chief of police and the city mayor stood to one side, glowering with anger and impatiently shifting from one foot to another. The fellow who offered his hand was dressed in a cutaway morning coat with a very large, diamond stickpin in his collar.

"Professor Bell, I presume. Welcome to our city. I am R. Beverly Cole, dean of the medical school and the city health officer. We have an unfortunate situation with an injured Chinaman named Chin Ten Sing. His physician refused our recommendation to perform trephination when he learned of your visit, and he insisted on waiting for you. The fellow believes in that damn Listerism," said Dr. Cole. Dr. Bell bristled, his features hardened.

"I was invited here to lecture on the antiseptic method and did not expect to have the method criticized," said Dr. Bell. I drew my jacket tighter against the cold fog, and out of the corner of my eye saw a slender, young man with oriental features standing well away from the group.

"See for yourself. The patient's physician is also a chink." said Dr. Cole.

"Gentlemen, this is not a time to quibble over medical matters. If the man dies, the chinks will riot and burn the city. Sir, we will appreciate anything you can do to help," the mayor said.

"I am happy to speak with the man. Will you kindly take Lady Penelope Walshingham and our baggage to the Palace Hotel?" asked Dr. Bell. Penelope flashed her usual come hither smile. Dr. Cole raised his hand, bowed, and whisked her into his elegant carriage.

I had the presence of mind to take up Dr. Bell's instrument case before we went to the waiting Chinaman. He bowed until the topknot of his cap almost touched the ground. Despite the cold, he wore a dark blue, silk blouse and pajama-like trousers. His hair hung halfway down his back in a single braid.

"Esteemed Dr. Bell, I am Lam Qua, physician to Chin Ten Sing. Please, kindly accompany me." Dr. Bell immediately plied him with questions.

"Who is this Chin Ten Sing?" asked Dr. Bell.

"He is my uncle and also the leader of the number one tong. One week ago, a gang of whites beat him senseless. He has not awakened since. If he dies, all Chinese will rise against the whites," said Lam Qua.

"How did you learn of Listerism?" asked Dr. Bell.

"I attended the mission school in Canton and assisted the doctor who was from the Yale University. He and my uncle, Chin Ten Sing, arranged for me to attend the Yale medical school. I learned of the antiseptic technique from the British medical journals. The doctors here do not believe in Lister," said Lam Qua.

We climbed into a curious conveyance, a cable car, similar to the one I had ridden before in Chicago, and went up Market Street to what I presumed was the border of Chinatown. A line of angry Chinese beat drums, clashed cymbals, and brandished hatchets at policemen, who were across the street. The police held revolvers cocked and ready to fire. A hundred or so rough-clad white men, armed with rifles and shotguns, threatened both the police and the Chinese.

"They are the militia," muttered Lam Qua.

Under the protection of Lam Qua, we scurried through an alley to a street festooned with yellow banners over shops of all kinds and description. It was a different, exotic world, unlike any I had seen. The roofs were of green tile, and the buildings were red and gold with carvings of dragons, lions, and murals of soft mountains wreathed with fog. We passed doors opening into small rooms where men lay on a dirty floor smoking small pipes. The air was filled with a sweetish smoke, which Lam Qua said was opium. The men wore the same type of blouse and pajama-trousers; some shuffled along with wicker baskets at each end of a bamboo pole held across their shoulders. Lam Qua knocked three times on a heavy, oaken door that was studded with iron bolts, until an elderly man with a wispy beard opened a small window next to the door. After a few words, the door opened. We passed through a large room filled with men playing with black and white buttons.

"A game of fan tan," Lam Qua informed us. We went through another heavy door also guarded by a look-out window into a room lavishly furnished with heavy, dark furniture, paintings, and a golden statue of a goddess. The place was heavy with incense, and at the end of the room, there was an enormous bed covered with a red, silk quilt. Two young women with smooth, black hair and cheeks tinged with red powder stepped aside as we approached the bed. At first, I could not be certain if the man was alive. He lay perfectly still; his hands, with skin like pale parchment, were folded over his chest on top of the silk quilt. His eyes were closed, and the yellowish skin of his face was nearly translucent. His eyes and cheeks were sunken. Most amazing of all, his scalp was clean-shaven except for a ragged patch of hair on the top of his head. There was a small bruise over his right ear. He has had nothing to eat or drink in three days," said Lam Qua.

Dr. Bell sat at the bedside and, with infinite care, lifted the patient's right wrist and placed his index finger on the pulse. "Tell me what happened."

"A gang of ruffians beat my uncle and cut off his queue. He has never regained consciousness. The American doctors recommended trephination," said Lam Qua.

"Why did they cut his hair?" asked Dr. Bell.

"Since the building of railroads has finished, there is no longer any need for Chinese. There is now a law against more Chinese coming to this country and the Americans want us to leave. We wear a queue, a long braid, as a sign of respect for our emperor, but the Americans have ordered us to cut our queues," said Lam Qua. At that moment, I distinctly thought I heard the old man sigh. Dr. Bell lifted the silk quilt and tapped the patient's knee tendon. There was a slight reflex response on both sides. He then stroked the soles of his feet. The great toe bent downward.

"A candle, please," said Dr. Bell. Lam Qua produced a lighted candle. Dr. Bell held open each eyelid and placed the candle directly in front of his face. Each pupil responded, equally.

He then sat silently, chin in hand, for almost ten minutes, before turning to me. "Arthur, what is your diagnosis?" he asked. I thought of all the usual causes for coma, drugs, head injury and diabetes but could not come up with an answer.

"The loss of his queue must have been a great shock. Please, my instrument case," said Dr. Bell. He removed the bear's tooth from a small compartment, placed it in the palm of Chin Ten Sing, and closed the old man's hand around the tooth.

"This is the tooth from a great and powerful bear. It is very strong medicine," said Dr. Bell. At that moment, I could have sworn our patient eyes fluttered and he took in a deeper breath.

"Lam Qua, explain to the women that they must prepare a soup with the necks and feet of two chickens, rice, and shredded ginseng root. They are to add this tooth to the soup." Dr. Bell said, with a faint smile.

Lam Qua eyes twinkled with delight. "Ah, your prescription will replace the power of the lost queue."

I was dumbfounded. Why was the professor, the epitome of scientific medicine, stooping to black magic? Professor Bell had held his finger on Chin Teng Sing's pulse during the entire time.

"My fee will be one hundred American dollars in gold eagles," Dr. Bell said, very loudly. This was most unusual. I had never heard Dr. Bell discuss his fee with a patient, but I knew better than to question him. Without a word, Lam Qua went to a brass, bound chest and removed five gold coins. He dropped them, one by one, in Dr. Bell's hand. *Clink, clink, clink, clink, clink.* At each *clink*, the old man's lips twitched.

"I shall return in two days," said Dr. Bell.

Lam Qua escorted us to the edge of Chinatown, where we hailed a hackney cab. "You are very perceptive," he said.

"Your treatment was most unusual," I said, when we were in the cab.

"My dear Arthur, it is elementary. The length of a Chinaman's queue is dear to his heart. Cutting the queue removes his sense of importance. When I mentioned the queue and the bear's tooth, his pulse rate increased, and it fairly leaped when I mentioned my fee. The old boy was wide awake and understood English. The cure will give him 'face' and he can brag that his treatment cost one hundred dollars. I shall see him again in two days," said Dr. Bell.

The streets were lined with aimless, ragged men, sitting on the sidewalk or leaning against a storefront looking out with vacant eyes. "Is it a holiday? Why aren't these men at work?" I asked.

"Ain't no work. The goldmines went bust, the railroads are built, and the damn slant-eyes work all day for nothin' but a bowl of rice," replied the driver.

We jogged along past shuttered shops and more ragged men. "The millionaires on Nob Hill gotta do something fast," said the driver.

The Palace Hotel, a vast, nine-story building of iron and brick loomed on Market Street. We drove in through the splendid, sky lighted garden court. There in the lobby, with his usual nonchalance, sat Mr. Sherlock Holmes, dressed, elegantly in fawn colored trousers, a white waist coat and a light blue frock coat.

I was flabbergasted. "How did you arrive before us?" I asked.

"The colonel arranged passage on a Navy ship, the 'Royal Sovereign from Portsmouth to New Orleans. From there, it was an easy journey by train," Holmes replied.

The lobby was swarming with doctors from all over the country, as well as stranded, eastbound travelers waiting for the railroad to open. Penelope, still in the traveling clothes she had worn since Denver, was in a towering rage. Not only was there no room for her, but the clerk refused to believe she was an English 'Lady.' Holmes already had a suite of rooms and the surgical association had reserved adjoining suites for me and Dr. Bell.

Penelope took my room and I moved in with Dr. Bell. We ascended to the ninth floor in a swell hydraulic elevator. Our rooms were equipped with every luxury, even an electric call button in case we needed a bootblack or refreshments. Dr. Bell hurried away to give his first lecture. I decided to accompany Penelope to a lady's haberdashery. The dear girl tried on evening dresses, day suits, frilly hats, sun bonnets and, behind closed doors, various undergarments. I was entranced by her transformation from a dusty, travel-stained woman to a real English lady. She preened and sighed and basked in my admiration, but I knew her too well to revive a romance. Still, she was bewitching and paid for the new outfit with the lucre she had won by betting on me and Mr. Wilde in Leadville.

Later, in his room, I recounted the murders and my own near death at the hands of the Russian count to Sherlock Holmes. He listened carefully, with his hands folded over his chest and his long legs extended on the fine carpet. When I finished the recital, he repeated my story word for word.

"There, do I understand you correctly?" he asked.

"Yes, indeed. You have grasped the situation."

26 June 1883, San Francisco

The morning clinic at the San Francisco City Hospital was an unexpected surprise. Here, at the very end of civilization, doctors were doing work which equaled that in Boston or Chicago. Dr. Bell fielded questions and demonstrated the antiseptic method on a jaw excision and a displaced fracture of the wrist in a twelve-year-old boy. The medical students and faculty from the medical division of the University of California were quite up to date except for a few holdouts who did not believe in the germ theory of disease. The third patient was a fifty-year-old man who worked as a coal stoker on a ferry boat. A medical student ushered him into the amphitheatre and tried to seat him on a chair, but with an enraged howl, the patient flung his arms and bared his teeth at the poor student. His face, pitted with old scars and marked with coal dust, was drawn back in a hideous rictus that exposed yellow teeth. He emitted animal-like moans and howls that expressed fear as much as rage. A woman with frazzled, grey hair and a lined face, who I presumed was his wife calmed him sufficiently that he took the chair for a moment. The patient's face, indeed his entire chest, was contorted with an effort to breathe. He would sit for a moment, but the paroxysms or spells would recur despite the best efforts of two medical students to restrain him. His mouth was dry, and he talked at great length but made no sense. I could only think of a strange form of epilepsy, criminal psychosis, or a brain tumor.

Dr. Levi Cooper, the senior surgeon who seemed to be very quick with the knife, advised an exploratory trephination searching for a tumor or blood clot. "Dr. Bell, do you agree with the need for surgery?" Dr. Cooper asked.

Dr. Bell observed the poor man with great intensity. "Nay. These movements are not convulsions. They are not lateralized to one side," said he. As if a light had flashed, his eyes twinkled. "Fetch a glass of water," he said. When the student returned, Dr. Bell held the tumbler in front of the patient's face. The poor man attempted a sip of water, but as soon as the liquid touched his lips, he made a most agonizing cry, clenched his lips, and attempted to strike Dr. Bell.

Dr. Bell sprang to one side, then took the wife's hand in his. "When did the dog bite your husband?" he asked.

"Never. We have no dog," she said. Dr. Bell, with a perplexed look on his face, again approached the patient and examined his hands and arms at length.

"What do you make of these marks on his right hand?" Dr. Bell asked.

"Sir, they are just scratches, certainly not important," said the student.

"When did the cat bite you?" asked Dr. Bell. The poor man clenched his teeth, and only after great difficulty did he respond.

"Tried to pet him, but he bit." Dr. Bell repeated the question to the man's wife. "Please, when did the cat bite your husband?"

Mebbe six weeks ago," the wife replied.

"If you please, take your patient to his room," said Dr. Bell. Two students led the patient and his wife away from the amphitheatre. "There we have it. The diagnosis is hydrophobia, also known as rabies. The ancients termed it 'the furious disease' and knew that venomous poison in the saliva of infected animals carried the disease. Dr. Louis Pasteur is working on a preventative vaccine but there is no hope for a cure. The best a mortal can do is make his life tolerable with morphine until death releases him from misery," said Dr. Bell.

The students applauded, and the attending physicians stood in line to shake Dr. Bell's hand and took him off to a luncheon.

29 June 1883, San Francisco

There is a gap since my last entry because so much has transpired, but I have not yet managed to remember it all. I took notes and made a sketch of the room during our visit to the Bohemian Club. Penelope has described some of the events and Dr. Bell filled in the remaining blanks in order to ensure that this entry is accurate.

I believe it was noon on the twenty-seventh when Lam Qua ushered me, Dr. Bell and Mr. Holmes into the inner sanctum where Chin Ten Sing sat, cross-legged, on a cushion before a low table. His merry eyes twinkled with delight when Dr. Bell made a slight bow. "Please be seated," said Chin Ten Sing. We sat on cushions and, with difficulty, crossed our legs beneath the low, polished table.

Our host clapped his hands. "Cha," said he. Instantly, a lovely girl with glistening, black hair and a body-clinging, silver-colored dress appeared with a tray. She knelt by the old man's side, deftly placed small cups on saucers before each of us, and put down a tea pot beside Chin Ten Sing. With his left hand, he poured tea for Dr. Bell, who sat on his left, and Lam Qua. Then, he pushed the pot to Lam Qua, who poured for me, Holmes and his uncle. This most delectable girl left and reappeared, then put plates on the table filled with tiny morsels of food. I was nonplussed because there was no knife, fork, or spoon. The girl returned and placed small trays containing slender sticks by each of us. While holding the sticks in one hand, Chin Ten Sing dexterously picked up a tiny steamed bun, tossed the morsel upwards, caught it in mid-air, and brought it to his mouth. Holmes imitated this amazing feat with an even tinier bit of fried shrimp. The Chinese looked on in amazement. Dr. Bell — noted for his dexterity with knife and forceps — attempted, without success, to pick up a tiny dumpling. Another delightful young lady, whose slit skirt showed a lovely leg, knelt by Dr. Bell and with great hilarity, demonstrated how to hold the chopsticks.

"Her name is Lotus Blossom," said Lam Qua. After a few minute's practice, I was able to pick up a small, steamed bun that contained delicious, barbecued pork. We ate shrimp dumplings, bits of pork, deep fried beef, and morsels of vegetables between slurps of delicious tea.

"Ah, you learn quickly. Catch this," said Chin Ten Sing, as he tossed a bit of fried prawn in the air. I missed, but Holmes managed to catch the morsel before it touched the table. Lotus Blossom clapped her hands, and laughed with a merry tinkle. She then swept away the dishes and returned with tiny cups, which she filled with a clear liquor poured from a porcelain bottle.

"You are English?" asked Chin Ten Sing.

"No, Scottish," Dr. Bell replied.

"But you have the same queen," said Chin Ten Sing.

"Yes, that is true," said Dr. Bell.

The old man raised his cup. "We drink to the English queen." I nearly choked. The liquid burned all the way down but left a warm feeling in the pit of my stomach. Lotus Blossom re-filled our cups. "it is rice brandy," she said.

Holmes raised his cup and spoke in what I later learned was Mandarin, "To the Emperor of China". The Chinese sucked in a deep breath.

"Where did you learn to speak Chinese?" Lum Qua asked.

"I spent several years in Tibet," Holmes replied.

"Does the English queen value her distant possessions and her people?" asked Chin Ten Sing.

"But of course," Holmes said.

"The Queen is very rich. She could pay well for information about a threat to her lands," said the old Chinaman. Dr. Bell carefully folded his hands on the polished surface of the table. His lids were half closed. Except for distant street noise, the room remained quiet.

"It would depend on the source and the reliability of the information," Holmes replied.

The old man took a sip of liquor and toyed with the tiny cup and then spoke in barely a whisper. "My nephew, Johnnie Chan, is number one boy in the house of Mr. Leland Stanford. Mr. Stanford thinks he is a stupid, illiterate Chinaman, but Johnnie studied in

Paris and knows English, as well as French. He has learned of a threat to the Queen's lands in Canada."

"We have great interest in the affairs of the Queen. We would appreciate any knowledge about threats to Her Majesty. Thank you for the lunch. I must give a lecture within the hour," said Dr. Bell. We made our bows, and again, Lam Qua escorted us to the edge of Chinatown. As if by magic, a skinny, bright-eyed boy of ten or twelve years appeared at my side.

"This is Pow Chan, my messenger," said Lam Qua. The small boy bowed and held out his hand with my wallet.

"I believe this belongs to you," he said.

"You picked my pocket!" I shouted. I wasn't sure whether to be impressed or horrified.

Lam Qua smiled. "Pow Chan is very talented and can be very helpful."

We walked for a while along Market Street, marveling at the sparkly day, the hills, and the vast bay.

Holmes lit up his meerschaum pipe and after a few puffs, we resumed our walk. "Chin Ten Sing is an old rascal who may or may not have useful information. This Stanford fellow offered Borovsky protection while you were in Boston. He is rich and powerful and may be working with Borovsky. Given what we know, and the fact that, at one time, the Russians claimed Northern California, we can assume the Russian is here in San Francisco. Miss Walshingham spent time with Borovsky; perhaps she has more information. We must take her in our confidence," Holmes said.

Dr. Bell went off to give a lecture, which I skipped since I had heard it many times. I invited Sherlock Holmes to our rooms to discuss the latest events with the Chinese. Penelope strutted into our suite as if she owned the hotel. She sniffed and gave me a back handed slap. "You have been with a Chinese floozy."

"A lovely Chinese girl served lunch for us and two Chinese gentlemen. You could take lessons in courtesy and female behavior," I said.

"You damn men are all alike."

"Now, Penelope, be a dear girl. Let's kiss and make up."

"Bah, why should I make up with a penniless doctor, even if you are handsome in a rugged sort of way?" It was her usual two-handed way of making me feel like a fool.

Holmes listened to our back and forth banter for a while. "Enough! Our Chinese friends think this Stanford fellow is plotting against the crown. Have you any leads on Jack Dawson or the Russian?" He asked.

Penelope smiled. It was one of her radiant, heart-throb-inspiring, appealing looks that I had succumbed to so often in the past. "What do you want?"

"Jack Dawson often mentioned the Bohemian Club. We might find him there or at least learn of his whereabouts," said Penelope.

"Why then, let us visit the place," Holmes said, with an exasperated sigh.

"It is a private, men-only club, mostly for newspaper men or literary types," said Penelope.

"Dress up in trousers, a shirt, a jacket, and a cap. You can pass for a man if you try," I said, rather jokingly.

The club was dingy, smoky, and filled with men wearing soft shirts, corduroy jackets, and with pencils stuck behind an ear. Most were at the bar. A few slurped oyster stew at wooden tables covered with checkered cloths. A huge fireplace dominated the room. From the mantelpiece, a wood carving of a one-eyed owl looked out over the crowd. We had no sooner gained entrance when a rough-looking fellow laid his hand on my collar. "You a member?" I was about to explain we were seeking guest privileges, when a voice bellowed a familiar poem.

Comrades, leave me here a little, while as yet 'tis early morn:
Leave me here, and when you want me, sound upon the bugle-horn .
. .

The speaker stopped for lusty drink from a tall glass. I responded with the next lines, which I knew by heart from having read them many times.

132

'Tis the place, and all around it, as of old, the curlews call,
Dreary gleams about the moorland flying over Locksley Hall.

We went on to the very end, reciting, in turn, all eighty-five or so stanzas of Tennyson's grand poem of lost love. At the end, my throat was dry. There were huzzahs and shouts of "More! More!" The rough fellow who had been set to throw us out thrust a whisky toddy in my hand and led us to a table. Holmes followed, seemingly puzzled at my literary ability. My fellow poet made his way to us through the throng and, with no invitation, flung himself into a chair. He wore a checked coat, a soft cap, and, for a fellow who had been tossing down whisky like it was water, was remarkably steady. I felt an immediate kinship with the man. He had the build of a rugby player, a ruddy face, a longish nose, and hooded eyes. He looked down his nose as if he were above it all.

"By God, you know Tennyson! I am Ian Blake, lately of Liverpool."

"Arthur Conan Doyle of Edinburgh, my good friend, Mr. Sherlock Holmes and my nephew, ah, David Doyle," said I, gesturing towards the newly-masculine Penelope.

"What brings you to our Paris of the Pacific?"

"A medical meeting. My professor is lecturing and demonstrating." He rubbed his jaw and cast what seemed to be a suspicious eye on Penelope.

"Are you one of the saw-bones who treated old Sing?" he asked.

"Yes," I answered.

"There are people here who want to see him dead. You might be in big trouble for interfering," Blake said.

"Why? He seems like a nice old man," I said.

Blake burst out laughing and took another pull at his whisky. "The old devil owns half of Chinatown and is standing in the way of the Nob's grand plans," he said.

"How so?" I asked.

"The workingmen hate the Chinese, and both the chinks and the working men are about to take down the Nobs."

"Who are the Nobs?"

Blake took a long drink before replying. "Oh, you are really a greenhorn. The millionaires who live on Nob Hill; Stanford, Crocker, Hopkins. The bastards made a fortune on railroads and mines. Now it is all bust, but they still have their millions and damn the rest. Stanford tells the Chinese he wants to hire them to build another railroad, and he tells the working man he will 'send the slant-eyes back' to China."

Holmes had sat quietly through this discussion but kept up his usual alertness. Penelope had sat with hands in her lap, eyes downcast. Blake suddenly grabbed her arm and pulled her hand into his lap. He leered at me, showing fine white teeth. "Such a delicate hand. Your nephew is more like a niece. Now, do you want to tell me what in Sam Hell you two are doing here?" he asked.

"If you must know . . ." I began, knowing it would be a lot worse if I didn't tell him the truth, "She is Lady Penelope Walshingham, traveling from England. A dastardly fellow named Jack Dawson robbed her of every cent, leaving her destitute. I am helping her find the wretch."

Blake winked and released his hold on Penelope. "If I know Dawson, he took more than her money."

"Do you know the man?" I asked.

"Half of California is looking for Jack. He staked every creek for miles around, then salted the area with fool's gold and a little dust. He let the suckers find a bit of gold, then sold the claims to gullible fools for thousands of dollars. He made a lot of money but lost most of it on cards and women. It is rumored that he is selling an Alaskan scheme to Stanford."

"Where can we find him?" Holmes suddenly asked.

"He may be hiding out with the Nobs, hatching a grand plan. I'll keep my eyes and ears open. Watch your back and be careful. My dear Penelope, I apologize if I grabbed your arm a bit too tightly. One can never be too sure who they are dealing with in these times, don't you think? Please, allow me to help with your grief over losing Dawson. My card," said he. He lifted Penelope's hand, looked around — as if to be sure no one was watching — placed a note in her palm, then gently closed her fingers around it before looking in her eyes and letting go. Though she watched his

134

every motion, Penelope stayed silent the whole time. I must admit I felt a pang of jealousy about his attentions, but I was also glad she was still there with me.

His card read:

IAN BLAKE
San Francisco Chronicle

Blake left our table to join another group. He was remarkably steady, and the thought passed my mind that he mostly drank watered-down booze in order to keep a sharp mind. Holmes watched him cross the room. "That man will be a great help in our endeavor. Let's go," Holmes said.

The night was cool, and dense fog obscured the buildings. No cabs were about, so we continued on foot, bumping into hitching posts and the occasional tree. We found our way to a recognizable landmark, the cast iron Lotta's Fountain. We set off on Market Street, arm in arm, not out of affection — at least on Penelope's part — but for protection. We had not gone far when a silent band of club-wielding men materialized out of the gloom. *Damn!* I thought. *My walking stick is back at the hotel.*

Before I could make a defense, one of the ruffians stifled Penelope's scream with a rough hand over her face. "Owee, he bit me!" howled her assailant. This was followed by a stifled moan when Penelope stabbed her elbow into his mid-section. I lashed out with a clenched fist. My wild haymaker struck a darkened face with enough force to break his jaw, but the fellow merely shook his head like a huge dog. I ducked when he swung a club at my noggin, but stumbled backwards against Penelope. The dear girl twirled and struck my assailant with the side of her hand. Much to my surprise, the fellow went down.

Holmes struck out with his fists, expertly knocking down several assailants, but there was no respite. Our fisticuffs and Penelope's martial arts skills were insufficient for conquering an entire gang. A powerful arm encircled my neck and twisted my entire head until I felt a *snap*, which was followed by a lightning bolt of pain in my legs. I went down, totally helpless, and my feet went numb, though I could still see. I was sufficiently conscious to wonder if this meant a broken neck and permanent paralysis. I expected another blow, but out of the misty gloom came a crowd of screaming dervishes led by a tall, shrouded, slender woman. She fired a pistol, and in the spurt of flame, I also saw the boy, who I recognized as Pow Chan, hurl a small hatchet. The picture is still there, engraved on my brain. The hatchet flew, end over end, until it split the skull of a burly, dark-faced villain. There were more hatchet-wielding, rock-throwing boys who came out of the foggy mist. Was it my imagination, or did the female figure look like Lotus Blossom? My immediate assailant went down with a bullet through his spleen. Another hatchet whistled through the air and split the head of a wild-faced ruffian. Another of our assailants snarled and struggled to his feet. A diminutive, pajama-clad figure sliced off two fingers of the wretch's right hand with a small hatchet.

"You bastids learn not to mess with triads." The voice was Pow Chan's.

My next conscious moment was an awareness of being gently lifted onto a litter and swiftly carried through dark, silent streets. Next came the sweetish odor of opium and the clacking sound of fan tan players. A door closed. There was absolute silence for a moment until a gentle hand caressed my forehead.

"You are safe," murmured a distant, musical voice. I drifted into a sort of stupor, but all the time was aware of tingling and numbness in both feet. With the greatest of will, I attempted to move my right leg, but I was unable to discern motion. Would I ever walk again? I have never felt more alone and desolate.

It could have been several hours or minutes until I recognized Lam Qua's calm words. "Do not move your head, but swallow these pills and drink," said he. The rice brandy burned all the way down, but I was soon drowsy and totally relaxed. I then had a vivid dream of walking through a bright meadow to dark woods. Even in my dream, I interpreted the dark woods as death but had no fear. At what seemed the very depth of the dream, I felt incredibly soft hands holding my shoulders while another set of hands slowly manipulated my head from side to side with increasing traction. The motion lulled me into another state of utter relaxation until the hands forced my head and neck backwards and to the right, at which time I felt my vertebrae snap. There was a great burst of light, and an incredible pain shot up the back of my head. I thought I screamed, but I can't be sure . . .

Next, I felt cold as ice and drifted off into the cold dark woods. I came out of the deep stupor with a sensation of warm flesh, a soft breast nestled against my chest. Nothing could have been more comforting. "Do not move," said Lotus Blossom. The pain was gone, but there was a tickling sensation on the sole of my right foot and a soft giggle when I jerked it way. *Glory be!* I wasn't paralyzed! I hungered for the continued warmth of her body, wanting to touch every part of this being who seemed to have magically brought me back to life. It was as if by feeling her aliveness, I was reconnecting with my own. I began to run my fingers through her hair, over her eyes, cheeks, and full lips, sliding over two lovely, soft nipples, a flat abdomen and a delicately indented navel.

"No monkey playing. You are poor, sick man. I am only warming your cold body so you live again," said Lotus Blossom. I sighed and attempted to sit up. "You be still until Lam Qua says you can move."

I must have slept again, and when I next awoke, my head and neck were immobilized in a padded scarf wrapped around my neck. I tentatively moved each arm and leg until I was quite satisfied there was no paralysis.

"You have good joss. Pow Chan was on the lookout for you. Lotus Blossom and the boys arrived in time. You will have no permanent injury," said Lam Qua. I was on a couch in a small, wood-paneled room lit with candles that smelled of incense. I felt a sense of great ease, which must have come from the opium, until bits and snatches of memory returned, bringing anxiety with them.

"Mr. Holmes and Penelope, what happened to Penelope?" I asked as the memory of the attack came more into focus.

"The English lady is quite safe in the hotel. Your friend Holmes has been here. He offered helpful suggestions on your treatment," said Lam Qua. I focused on Lotus Blossom, grateful she had brought me back to life. How much more was there than I first thought to this beautiful, slender girl who taught me to use chopsticks and then saved my life? Could she also be the leader of a deadly gang?

Lam Qua must have understood my silent curiosity. "Lotus Blossom is the most fragrant flower of all of Chin Ten Sing's 'nieces.' She is also known as the Tooth of the Dragon or simply, the Dragon Lady, one who has become both a great healer and warrior woman," said Lam Qua.

I have a dim recollection of being given another pill, a brown one, and a glass of the fiery rice brandy, then being strapped onto a litter and carried again through the streets and an alley, through a dim back door, and up several flights of stairs. When I awoke, I was in my own bed in the hotel suite. Dr. Bell was at my bedside.

"What is the date?" I asked.

"June the twenty-ninth," replied Dr. Bell. "My boy, you have had quite a night."

He wore his ancient, red dressing gown, was surrounded by newspapers, medical journals, and his notebook, and was intensively studying a map of San Francisco. Clouds of fragrant smoke rose from his favorite calabash. "I suspect you are hungry," Bell said.

"Ravenous." I found I could rise from bed, though still felt shaky, weak, and sore in every joint and muscle. I haltingly made my way to the table, which was laden with boiled eggs, ham, smoked salmon, a dish of oat porridge, and a gallon-sized pot of coffee. Though I was still foggy-headed and ate slowly, I managed to finish every crumb.

"Where is Penelope?" I asked, after feeling my energy slowly starting to return.

Dr. Bell tamped more tobacco into his pipe, struck a lucifer, and puffed until the tobacco was a glowing, red coal. "Read this." He handed a page of plain, lined foolscap with a message. It was in Dr. Bell's own handwriting. "I translated this coded cable an hour ago."

Mr. Sherlock Holmes to take over the investigation, remain in S.F. until situation resolved. Holmes to employ Lady Walshingham as he sees fit. Agent will make contact. Edwards.

I mused over the message. The colonel had apparently followed our adventures. Bell rang for the valet, who appeared almost instantly.

The bright eyed young man wore the elaborate hotel uniform and readily accepted two silver dollars. "If you please, request Lady Walshingham and Mr. Sherlock Holmes to join us for tea at their convenience. Holmes and Penelope arrived almost together within an hour.

"This is no time for tea, I have arranged for strong coffee," Dr. Bell said. He then handed the message to Sherlock Holmes, who in turn passed the paper to Penelope.

"Yes, I am quite prepared," Holmes said. He gave Penelope an appraising look and then withdrew from an inside pocket a package of Sobraine cigarettes. "A small token of our future. Miss Walshingham, do you have a command of the French language?"

Penelope sniffed, "Off course and Russian and German."

"Good, I have a task for you, right in the enemy's nest."

Holmes unfolded a newspaper to a page with personal advertisement.

"Wanted, private tutor for young man. Must speak French. Room, board and a stipend of twenty-five dollars per week.

This advertisement is for the young son of Leland Stanford. Miss Walshingham your first task is to answer this advertisement, in person and make yourself invaluable to the boy.

"The young Stanford, an only child boy will accompany his parents on a grand tour of the continent next year. You will help convert him into an English gentleman, and teach him fluency in French and Russian. According to the advertisement, you will have comfortable quarters in the Stanford mansion on Nob Hill. You will report any news of Borovsky," Holmes said.

The room was silent, while we attended to strong black coffee and breathed nicotine. Great clouds of tobacco smoke hung in the air, like a fog over the bay.

Dr. Bell broke the silence. "With Holmes on the job, I can attend to medical affairs. Come, Doyle do you feel well enough to accompany me on a consultation? I suggest you take the various armaments provided by the colonel, as a precaution," Dr. Bell said. I was still somewhat befuddled but instantly became interested. Dr. Bell's consultations always led to new adventures.

"Yes, of course, I feel well enough. What is the case?" I asked.

"A military problem," he answered, with a mysterious little smile.

We set off in a hired cab. The day was marvelously clear, and as we came down the hill, we were treated to a remarkable view of the bay, islands, and along the foreshore, the hulks of innumerable ships. The cab driver explained that these were windjammers that had rounded Cape Horn from the east coast of the United States to California during the gold rush. The crews jumped ship to search for gold, leaving the abandoned ships. "There appear to be workers on some of the ships," I said. The driver squinted at the partly refurbished ships.

"Those 'uns be bought by the Occidental and Oriental Steamship line. Old Leland's got no more use for the Chinese and figures on sending them home, but them ships'll go down afore they reach the Farallones," said the cabby.

We went through Cowtown, a dismal neighborhood, turned onto Presidio Drive, and arrived at a military base. We trotted through a delightfully wooded meadow overlooking the bay, where curving streets were lined with barracks for enlisted men, bungalows for the lieutenants, and mansions for high-ranking officers. Artillery pieces aimed at the bay dotted the landscape.

"Here be Fort Point," said the cabby. We alighted before the stone and brick building, which was guarded by a single, slouching sentry whose boots and rifle were dirty. He barely acknowledged Dr. Bell's request to see Captain Hennessey, the medical officer. The sentry slouched along, dragging his rifle and led us to a small infirmary.

"The American military lacks British discipline," Dr. Bell said.

"Aye, they have no one to fight, now that they have subdued the Indians."

Captain Hennessey sat hunched over a littered desk in a small office. Cabinets contained medical equipment, including a scalpel still smeared with pus. Bookshelves lined the walls. The medical officer was bleary-eyed and had dirt beneath his fingernails. With seemingly great effort, he roused himself from a padded chair.

"Gentlemen, thank you for arriving so promptly."

"Always delighted to see an interesting diagnostic problem," Dr. Bell replied. "Orderly, fetch Duncan and Hancock," shouted Captain Hennessey.

Duncan, a sergeant, and Hancock, a corporal, were battle-scarred veterans well into their forties. "These white spots have me puzzled," said Hennessey. Duncan thrust out his hands. Although his face was tanned a deep mahogany brown, the skin of his hands showed blotchy patches of de-pigmentation that were pronounced on the ulnar side. Dr. Bell inspected each of his hands, first with his naked eye, then with a small hand lens. Without a word, he removed a pin from behind the collar of his jacket and pricked the skin of each hand.

"Ouch!" said Duncan, when the pin pricked his index finger.

Dr. Bell paused for a moment, then drove the pin deeply in to one of the white spots. The soldier made no response. "Did that hurt," Dr. Bell asked. "Didn't feel a damn thing," Duncan said.

I instantly knew the diagnosis. Dr. Bell remained expressionless but nodded at Corporal Hancock who thrust both hands forward. Dr. Bell again carefully scrutinized a small, white patch and then felt the ulnar nerve at the patient's elbow.

"How long has the nerve been swollen?" Dr. Bell asked.

"Bout six months, more or less," said the corporal.

"When were you men out of the country?" Dr. Bell asked.

"Back in '78 to '80, I was a guard at the legation in Shanghai," said Hancock.

"I had duty in the Sandwich Islands from '79 to 81," said Duncan.

"Thank you, gentlemen, that will be all," said Dr. Bell.

141

"Dismissed!" barked the orderly.

Dr. Bell folded his hands. His face was set in a hard line when he finally spoke.

"The diagnosis is leprosy."

Hennessey recoiled. "No, that's not possible. They are white men. The chinks get it from opium and filth," said he.

"Hanson, a Swedish scientist, has definitely demonstrated leprosy to be caused by a germ that is passed from one person to another. You can prove the diagnosis by scraping the skin and applying the proper bacterial stains," said Dr. Bell.

"You say it is contagious?" Hennessy asked.

"Yes. I advise you to examine every man on the base," replied Bell.

"Does this mean quarantine?" Hennessey asked.

"Indeed, it does," replied Bell.

Hennessy put his head in his hands. "The colonel won't like this, but it won't make a hell of a lot of difference. Half the garrison has syphilis and the rest are down with scurvy. The government doesn't give a damn about the army anymore," he said. The ride and the day's exertions left me with a recurrence of pain and slight weakness in my left foot. I am tired and still recovering, so I was glad it turned out there was no need for armaments. We have returned to our rooms and, though it is early in the day, I am ready to collapse into bed.

30 June 1883

I slept for the remainder of the day and night and awoke this morning with some aches and pains, but felt much better than yesterday. Dr. Bell had left, probably for another consultation, by the time I awoke. There was an envelope with my name — written in precise, perfect penmanship — on the breakfast tray. A note read: *If you please, Pow Chan will meet you and Mr. Sherlock Holmes at noon and guide you to Ah Toy's House of Pleasure for lunch. Lam Qua*

I adjusted the ankle sheath for my stiletto, dressed with care, placed the brandy flask in an inside pocket, and took up the walking stick. I felt a bit ridiculous with these armaments, but this time, I will be prepared for any eventuality. Along with my anxiety, there was tingle of anticipation. Perhaps, the lovely Lotus Blossom attend the luncheon?

Near the hotel entrance, a small boy, whose features were obscured by dirt and a large straw hat, was polishing the boots of a well-dressed gentleman. When finished, the man withdrew a large wallet from an inside coat pocket and flipped a coin to the boy, replaced the wallet, and selected a cigar. The boy immediately struck a lucifer and held the flame to the cigar. While the man rotated the cigar to achieve a perfect glow, the boy, with his other hand, deftly removed the wallet. In the twinkling of an eye, the boy, whom I recognized as Pow Chan, squatted on the cobblestones before me.

"Polish your boots," said he. The large gentleman, now unknowingly bereft of his wallet, was already in a cab, trotting down the street.

"You little rascal," I said.

Holmes, with a twinkle in his eye pointed to a pair of pigeons. "Watch the birds," he cried and with a slight of hand, slipped the wallet from Pow Chan's pocket. When the boy turned back, his face broke in to a broad grin. "Ah, you better than Chinese," he said. Holmes returned the wallet. I continued to marvel at Holmes many skills. Pow Chan beckoned us to follow.

He set off at a fast pace to Grant Street, passed the Kow Chow temple, and stopped at a large, red door.

"Fifty-six Ross Alley," said Pow Chan. He rapped three times, paused, and gave two more taps. An elderly man opened a small window, and after they exchanged a few words in Chinese, he admitted us to an ante-room and then a second room, which smelled of incense and was decorated with dragons and paintings of temples.

A strikingly tall, beautiful woman wearing a clinging skirt, slit to her thigh, hobbled on bound feet across the room. "Welcome to the house of Madam Ah Toy." Lam Qua and Lotus Blossom rose from the low table where they had been seated prior to our arrival.

"Welcome. Meet Johnny Chan," said Lam Qua. Chan was tall, had black hair combed straight back from a high forehead, and was dressed in fashionable western clothing. He gave us an imperious, hostile glance and made no greeting. It was hard to believe he was the house boy for Leland Stanford.

"Please, be seated," said Lam Qua. When we were settled on cushions around the low table, Madam Ah Toy clapped her hands. Servants appeared with tiny cups and pots of bitter tea. After the tea, they brought trays filled with small, delectable bits of meat, fish, shrimp, and tiny dumplings. I wolfed down pork spiced with garlic. Holmes with his usual grace and dexterity picked out the smallest bites with chopsticks.

"My girls' lonesome. No soldiers come last night," sighed Madam Ah Toy. Johnny Chan gave me a look of pure hatred.

"Then it is true. The American soldiers cannot leave the Presidio. Very bad for business in Chinatown. Uncle Sing and tongs are very unhappy," Johnny Chan said.

"You English doctors do this?" asked Madam Ah Toy.

"This could be very bad. With no American Army, the California Militia will be the only military in the state," said Lam Qua.

"This is not good for Chinese. The English doctors must rescind the order and let the soldiers go free." said Chan.

"Leprosy is contagious. It is necessary to protect the community," Holmes said.

"Ha, you only protect the whites on Nob Hill," said Chan. We continued eating in silence, and when we had consumed the last bits of dim sum and the servants had cleared away the dishes, Johnny Chan rose to his feet and commenced speaking in rapid-fire Chinese.

Lam Qua raised a hand. "Johnny, please speak English for our guests."

Chan's face turned into an angry scowl. "The English dogs are no friend of our emperor and have no business here. They do nothing for us."

"The Americans are our enemies. We have a common cause with the English," said Lam Qua.

Johnny Chan's angry retort was blocked by shouting and the sound of gunfire from the street. The screams and cries became more distinct. "It is the California Militia," said Lam Qua. The crackling rifle shots were closer and louder.

"They have come for my girls!" screamed Madam Ah Toy. The heavy oak and bolted doors were no match for heavy axes. The outer door opened with a crash, and when the inner door to our room trembled with powerful blows, we scrambled to the narrow stairway that led to the kitchen. Madam Ah Toy tripped on her bound feet, fell, and blocked the exit. For a moment, I crushed Lotus Blossom in my arms, then thrust her behind Johnny Chan. As if in a dream, I remembered Colonel Beachy-Edwards words, "flash" and "bang." I hastily withdrew the brandy flask, and just as a half dozen crazed militia men crashed through the door, I gave the lid a twist, counted to three, and threw the flask. It landed in the midst of the intruders. The flask went off with a *bang* and a *whoosh*. The room filled with a yellow, acrid smoke that drove the militia back into the ante-room. Holmes stood his ground, withdrew a small revolver from an inner pocket and fired a series of shots. There were howls of pain. Johnny Chan led us to a narrow winding stairway to the kitchen, then down another flight of stairs into a subterranean room that connected with an adjacent building. "Here, I leave you," Chan said.

"Follow me," said Lam Qua. We found our way through a series of rooms hidden beneath the buildings until we exited on Grant Street at the edge of the Chinese district.

"You go to office of Mr. Ian Blake at the Chronicle. Tell him what happened," said Lam Qua. The gunfire had subsided, and the streets were clear as we made our way to the newspaper office. Blake's office was a cluttered cubbyhole redolent with old tobacco smoke. Holmes sniffed like a bird dog and folded himself in to an empty chair.

"We meet again," Blake said.

"A gang of white men from the militia stormed the Chinese district," I said.

"I heard the gunfire. It happens every month or so."

"Damn! Why do they do that? They are murdering innocent people," I said. Blake twirled a pencil between his fingers and gave me a long, speculative look. He slammed the door but we could easily hear conversations in the next office through the flimsy walls.

Blake drew up chairs chair. "*Nos socii. Pater noster est Beachy*," said he. Holmes immediately translated; "We are partners. Our father is Beachy. Now, explain, what the devil is going on,"

Blake lowered his voice to a near whisper. "I keep an eye on the British interests. The Nobs need only the slightest excuse to take over the entire Pacific coast from Alaska to California."

"Would a huge discovery of gold and other minerals in the Yukon be a sufficient excuse?" Holmes asked.

"Yes, a big strike would be the perfect excuse," said Blake. He shuffled through a stack of paper. "Ah, here it is. Stanford and his associates have proposed building a railroad through British Columbia and the Yukon to Alaska. The British rejected the proposal. The Americans don't think Alaska has anything of value. Stanford must have inside information about the gold and minerals," said Blake.

"Why is Johnny Chan angry with us?" I asked.

"It is a sad story. Chan came with his father to work on the railroads. He carried spikes when he was ten years old. His father became ill, couldn't work, and a foreman beat him to death. Old

Chin Ten Sing took care of Johnny. Chan is brilliant but hates all whites," said Blake.

"Get him! Stop the little bastard!" The shouts in the outer office were accompanied by a clatter of overturned chairs and broken glass. The door to Blake's office burst open. Pow Chan tumbled into the room.

"Lotus Blossom hurt … Come quick!" he shouted.

We followed Pow Chan through the streets to a tiny storefront on a dirty alley just off Grant Street. Johnny Chan cradled Lotus Blossom in his arms while an old lady held a compress on her neck. "They shot her," said Chan. She was unconscious, her skin was blue, and she wasn't breathing. I looked more closely to see how badly she was injured. The bullet appeared to have entered near the midline in front of her neck and exited at the left side.

"Where is Dr. Lam Qua?" I asked.

"The damn militia hurt many people. He is in the streets rescuing the wounded," said Chan. When I removed the compress, there was a torrent of blood. She should have been pale from blood loss, not cyanotic. Pressure on the wound stopped the external bleeding. I pictured the anatomy but it was Holmes, the master anatomist who shouted, "The bullet went through her trachea. She has bled into her lungs."

"Quick, hold her upside down!" said I. Johnny Chan gave me a questioning look, but obeyed and suspended the girl so her head and upper body hung down. I flung both arms around her chest and gave a great hug, released my pressure and gave a second squeeze as hard as possible. A great torrent of clots and blood erupted from her mouth. Lotus Blossom made a convulsive gasp, took in air, and coughed out more gouts of blood. I squeezed again. She coughed, more blood drained from her mouth, and she took in a long, gurgling gulp of air.

"Put her on the counter," Holmes said. Chan swept aside boxes of tea, dried fish, and vegetables in order to create a space for Lotus Blossom.

"Tell Pow Chan to find Dr. Bell," Holmes said. I held the compress for half an hour until a half-dozen ragged, little boys with

Dr. Bell charged into the room. The boys chattered all at once, and Pow Chan proudly carried the instrument case.

"I am compressing the jugular vein. She had blood in her trachea," I said. Dr. Bell took in the situation and, with his usual aplomb, removed his coat, rolled up his sleeves, and placed an assortment of gleaming forceps, knives, scissors, and ligatures on a towel. He rinsed his hands and soaked a gauze compress with carbolic.

Lotus Blossom moaned and attempted to raise an arm. "A few drops of chloroform will not be amiss. Mr. Holmes, if you please, give the anaesthetic," said Dr. Bell. At the first whiff of chloroform, she stopped breathing and her eyes rolled back. Holmes placed his lips on hers and forced air into her lungs. She revived. I kept pressure on the vein while Dr. Bell made an incision connecting the entrance and exit wounds. I have never seen such a deft bit of workmanship. The tissues were suffused with blood, but with unerring skill, he encircled the torn vein with ligatures and stopped the bleeding. He cleaned the area with carbolic swabs and sutured a bit of muscle against the perforated trachea.

"She will live," said Dr. Bell.

"I will take her to the home of Chin Ten Sing," said Chan. He looked from Holmes to me. "You are indeed good friends."

We followed Pow Chan to the Kow Chow Temple, where Lam Qua patched the wounds of blood-splattered victims. We spent the rest of the day working with the wounded.

1 July 1883, San Francisco

Our leisurely breakfast was interrupted by a knock on the door. The bellboy, dressed in an impeccable scarlet uniform, bowed. "A message for Dr. Bell." Dr. Bell put down his cup and read the penciled note. *An interesting autopsy. Medical school auditorium, ten o'clock a.m. R. Beverly Cole, MD*

We arrived just as the deaner, assisted by a student, rolled a pale, naked body into the auditorium and placed it on a table directly in front of the tiers of students. Holmes and Ian Blake were with the students in the front row.

Greasy, grey intestines spilled out of a great slash down the front of the body. The eye sockets were empty. Birds had evidently pecked out the eyeballs. I gasped, covered my mouth, and averted my eyes from the body. I recognized the long, sandy hair that I had once attempted to pull from Jack Dawson's skull. Dr. Cole bustled into the room wearing a blood-stained apron over his fashionable frock coat.

"The ferry boat men found him floating in the bay yesterday afternoon." He nodded to Dr. Bell. "You have never seen the likes of this in Scotland, I'll wager. Would you care to examine the body?" asked Dr. Cole. He strutted about like a pompous jay, obviously intent on showing up Dr. Bell before the students.

Dr. Bell chin in hand, observed the body but said nothing.

"Well, what do you make of it?" asked Cole. I had averted my eyes from the awful scene, but when Cole spoke, I looked more closely. The left hand had been amputated at the wrist and it was held with a spike, which had been driven through the hand and into his chest. Dr. Bell stooped and examined the hand.

"This is most peculiar; the thumb is extended up towards the chin, the three middle fingers are curled inwards, and the fifth finger is aimed downward," said Dr. Bell.

"Well, doctor, do tell us . . . What is the meaning of the hand?" asked Dr. Cole.

Dr. Bell shook his head. "I have never seen the likes of it."

Mr. Sherlock Holmes stepped down from the gallery and with his usual care examined the body. "Gentlemen, the upraised

149

thumb represents the head of a dragon and the fifth finger the tail. This is the work of the Chinese triads. I will prove it. The man's gallbladder will be absent." He bowed to Dr. Cole. "See for yourself, sir. Cole delved into the abdomen. "Yes, you are quite right. The gallbladder is missing. "The fiends drink the gall of their enemies for strength," said Holmes.

"Are you quite certain the man was dead before he was thrown into the water?" asked Holmes.

"Yes, of course," said Cole.

Holmes smiled at the students. "At times, the truth is not found at first appearances. Note the bulging spaces between the ribs on the left side, while the right, intercostal spaces are normal," He said. Holmes then placed his middle finger on the chest wall and thumped it with his other index finger. The sound was a dull *thud*.

"Gentlemen, if indeed the man was dead when he entered the water, the lungs should be full of air. What explains the dullness to percussion and the bulging intercostal spaces?" asked Holmes. . The students shuffled their feet, but no one had an answer.

"What is this damn nonsense?" asked Cole.

"Mr. Holmes has made an important discovery. If you please, Dr. Doyle, turn the body over to expose the back," said Dr. Bell. I took the shoulders and stared into the distorted face of Jack Dawson. I could barely stifle a cry. I had disliked the man, but hadn't wished for his death.

"Please, Dr. Doyle, assist me," Dr. Bell said. I swallowed bile and, with the aid of a student, rolled the body onto the abdomen. There was a small stab wound in the upper left chest.

"Bah, that little wound could have been a fish bite," said Dr. Cole.

"A knife, please," Holmes said. He made a deep incision down to the ribs and spent a few minutes removing a segment of rib. The students fidgeted and Dr. Cole hopped about.

"Damn it. The cause of death is plain as the nose on your face. The triad killed him," Dr. Cole said.

Holmes paid him no attention and cut deeper until he encountered blood clots in the chest cavity. "Forceps, please." Holmes withdrew a sharpened, white bone from the mass of clotted blood. The students gasped, and I was immediately awestruck by another of his triumphs.

"It is a spear point from a harpoon. I saw many of them when I sailed on the *Hope* in the Arctic!" I cried.

Holmes held the bloody spear point for all to see. "Here is the cause of death. This spear point penetrated the pulmonary artery. Indeed, this point is a weapon used by the Arctic Eskimo. Here is the toggle that releases the shaft of the harpoon," he said.

Dr. Bell Mr. bowed to the students. "Mr. Holmes has demonstrated how a simple bedside diagnostic technique can be applied to solving forensic problems and how in your practices, you will often be led astray by first appearances. Observe closely. Search out every detail before you make a diagnosis. In this case, the murderer attempted to fasten blame on the Chinese." The students clapped and stomped their feet, while Dr. Cole hurriedly left the auditorium.

"May I treat you gentlemen to lunch?" asked Ian Blake.

"Our pleasure," said Dr. Bell.

Pow Chan and his collection of scabby, little boys were playing dice beneath a tree when we came out of the medical school. Pow Chan waved them away and trotted after us while we walked to Powell Street and boarded the Powell-Hyde cable car for a ride down the hill to a busy collection of wharfs, piers, and boat landings. A cluster of small fishing boats was docked at a long wharf, and others were anchored in the bay. Gulls, cormorants, and terns flew and squawked as we made our way along the waterfront to a ramshackle building with a sign, 'Restaurante Italiano.'

"Achilles Paladine is the fish king," said Blake. Paladine, a weather-beaten man with a huge, drooping mustache, embraced Blake at the door.

"Welcome, my fren'. You want the usual place?" he asked.

"Yes," said Blake. We went up a narrow stairway to a room containing a single table that overlooked the Golden Gate. We were scarcely settled at a round table covered with a checked cloth when a young man arrived bearing a jug, long loaves of crisp bread, and small dishes of olive oil. Blake poured red wine from the jug and tore off chunks of bread that he dunked in the olive oil.

"Help yourselves," said he.

Next came a platter of shellfish and a bowl of melted butter. "Dungeness Crab," said Blake. He broke open a long claw and extracted white meat. One of the most satisfying aspects of our travels in America is feasting on the diverse foods. For the next thirty minutes, we gorged on the succulent crab, prawns, fish, and bowls of creamy noodles spiced with herbs and tomato sauce.

It was late afternoon before waiters swept away the remnants of our feast and left a pot of coffee. "Perhaps, I should establish my bonafides," said Blake. He placed on the table one third of a bronze penny. I stared at a part of the face of young Queen Victoria and the word, 'VICTOR.' The rest was missing. Holmes placed another third of the coin next to that of Blake's. It matched perfectly.

"Where is the other third?" I asked.

"Lady Walshingham," said Holmes.

I could hardly contain my inward rage. There were many instances, during our travels to America and Russia, in which I had given my time, and nearly my life, for the Crown. Yet, my loyalty seemed to go unappreciated.

"Why don't I have a part of the coin? Have my efforts on behalf of the Crown these last five years meant nothing? Penelope is someone known to be untrustworthy; a double, if not triple, agent. Why would she be the one to have that honor?" I asked.

"You are indeed a valued member of our group, but Colonel Beachy-Edwards could not know for certain if you would accompany me on this trip. He has implicit faith in Lady Walshingham and entrusted her with the final third prior to your invitation to join us," said Bell.

Though not fully satisfied with his answer, I was slightly mollified.

"Do you know who killed Jack Dawson?" Blake asked.

Holmes fussed with his pipe and tobacco until he blew a perfect ring of smoke. "The weapon is of Eskimo origin," said he.

"There are no Eskimos in the entire state of California," said Blake.

"The harpoon point is the type of artifact that an explorer would collect. Now that I think of it, Count Borovsky was a member of the Russian-Alaska Company," I said.

Dr. Bell arched his eyebrows. "Count Borovsky is very clever. Had it not been for Arthur's quick work, we never would have suspected that man's foul play in the murder of the twins. Yes, this could most certainly be the work of Borovsky."

"Dawson stole Borovsky's case of specimens, so the count had a motive," I said.

Blake gestured at a black-hulled ship with three masts and a funnel. An ensign with the Saltire of St. Andrews and a Maltese cross flew at the stern. "That Russian warship has been here for two weeks. Most Russians have left the bay area, but there is a large colony at Fort Ross, up the coast. At one time, they claimed all of Northern California. The Russians are indeed up to no good," said Blake.

"Why would the killer want us to blame Dawson's murder on the Chinese?" I asked.

"It would be an easy diversionary tactic. Unfortunately, because the Chinese are different, or seem exotic, and Americans think they are taking jobs, they are believed to be sinister and are easy scapegoats for everything bad," said Blake.

We had been silent for some time, savoring the last of our strong Italian coffee and watching the last rays of sunlight reflected from a mass of clouds over the Golden Gate. Out of the dusk came three identical ships with four masts, square sails, high sterns, and forward cabins. The ships were festooned with red pennants bearing Chinese characters, and a great bronze cannon was mounted mid ship on the lead vessel.

"What strange ships," I said.

"They are ocean-going, Chinese junks that make the round trip from Shanghai twice a year. They always come in just before dark, when the customs inspectors have gone home." said Blake.

"Why?" I asked.

"The Chinese Exclusion Act bars more Chinese from entering the country, so the men have no women. Chin Ten Sing buys women in China and smuggles them into San Francisco. Their families get money that is needed for their survival and they have the opportunity for a new life in America. The youngest and prettiest wind up in Madam Ah Toy's brothel and the rest he sells to men. It is the only way for the men to have Chinese wives. He also smuggles opium," said Blake.

"Can't the Americans put a stop to it?" I asked.

"Tonight, every woman and every bit of opium will be loaded into small fishing boats and will be gone. When the custom officials inspect tomorrow, they will find only bolts of silk, dried fish, and Chinese trinkets. You should not be surprised. Old Sing bought the lovely Lotus Blossom in Shanghai. She is now his number one concubine," said Blake. I almost choked on my coffee. I could not imagine dear Lotus Blossom in the arms of that old man. I am not sure I would have advocated saving him if I had known he was keeping her as if she was a slave. The more I thought about it, the more irate I became.

"The man is a slaver, a damn criminal!" I shouted.

Blake fiddled with a black, twisted cigar for a moment. "No. It is seen as a service to the Chinese since it is the only way for the men to have women and start a family. The women are better off here than in China, where they would starve. Lotus Blossom is fortunate and has great status here. Some people say she is a Lung Tao, or Dragon Head, in the Precious Tiger Society. In China, she would have suffered a worse fate," said Blake.

"What is the Precious Tiger Society?" I asked.

"The society is an ancient Chinese triad, a network of arch-criminals. Here, they run the opium dens and the cheaper brothels. They rarely become involved in affairs outside of Chinatown, but that may change," said Blake.

I have had the bad habit of falling in love with nearly every beautiful woman I encounter. As with many of those before, I knew the idea of possibly starting a romance with Lotus Blossom was a mere fantasy, but I still felt an emptiness at hearing this news. Even though she appeared to be well-respected, it didn't seem like this turn of events gave her a fair chance at a decent life of her own choosing. I could take her away from all of this, but would she be happy in Edinburgh? What was I feeling for her, anyway? Was it love, or was it just the wine talking?

2 July 1883, San Francisco

Despite the events of the last few days and the sense of deflation I felt yesterday upon learning about Lotus Blossom, today started as a delightful morning. I figured it would be good to get some fresh air, so I took my camera and decided on a solitary stroll to photograph the astounding sights in this grand city. In the hotel lobby, a dumpy, middle-aged lady poked me with an umbrella. I did not recognize Penelope until I heard her voice.

"Meet me at the ferry landing," she said. I went out into bright sunshine, and after a half a block, I glanced back. Penelope wore a long, grey dress. A black shawl covered her head and shoulders. She appeared heavy around the middle, had a curious hump on her back, and waddled as if her feet hurt. I waited at the ferry ticket office until she caught up, and separately, we made our way to seats on the upper deck. Her hair was darker with streaks of grey, her cheeks were puffy, and her glorious bosom was flattened. We said nothing until the ferry was well out into the bay. Engine noise, the cry of gulls, and the wind swept away the sound of our voices.

"Mr. Holmes did the disguise and it is a good thing. I saw Borovsky," said Penelope.

"Where?" I asked.

"In Stanford's library. He claims to be a direct envoy from the tsar," she said.

"Then he really could have been the one who killed Dawson," said I.

"Dawson was of no importance. Borovsky got to Stanford first."

"Start at the beginning.

"I took the job to teach Stanford's son French and Russian. He is a smart boy, an only child, and learns fast. We got along well, and within a couple of days, I had the run of the house. One evening, when the family was away, I slipped into Stanford's private office. The house boy, a big Chinaman, grabbed me around the neck and held a knife to my face."

"Johnny Chan?" I asked.

"Yes. First, he asked if I knew you. When I reassured him, he asked me to set up a meeting with you for today," said Penelope.

We followed wagons and carriages off the ferry to the Alameda landing. Penelope pointed south, along the shore. "A half-mile past the marine railway, look for a boat flying a flag with a green turtle." Penelope gave me a cool kiss and left the way we had come. I walked along a muddy, rutted road past an industrial shipyard and fishing boats tied to crumbling wooden docks until I saw the flag with a green turtle at the masthead of a small fishing boat. It was about forty feet long, flat-bottomed with a high stern, and tied to a crumbling, wooden dock. A dark-skinned Chinaman, wearing a straw hat with a conical crown and pajama pants cut off at his knees, squatted at the bow. He motioned for me to board, held out his hand, and I clambered onto the deck. The Chinaman grinned and pointed to the midsection that was partially enclosed by a curved bamboo overhead. I did not recognize Johnny Chan until he spoke.

"Sit here." Chan also wore dirty pajamas and a large straw hat that hid his features. The man at the bow shoved off, while another at the stern sculled the boat offshore with a long oar. When crewmen raised a huge, rectangular sail, the wind sent us skimming across the bay.

"Wear this," said Chan. I put on one of the straw hats and a dirty cloak that covered my western clothing. We were heading southwest towards the southern part of San Francisco. "There is Potrero Point and, over there, Hunters Point," said Chan, as he pointed out both locations. I made out a mass of smokestacks, dark, low buildings, and a locomotive. When we drew closer, I could see a huge dry dock occupied by a two-funnel steamship. Chan uncased a long brass telescope. "Take a good look," he said. At first, I focused on a low, sandy beach and swampland that rose to low hills. There, men were pushing carts, and steam-powered trucks scuttled about on tracks. It was a busy industrial complex. "That is the Union Iron Works, manufacturers of locomotives, mining equipment, and rolled steel. Further along is the shipyard," said Chan.

"It is huge," I said.

"It is the largest industrial complex of any Pacific nation. Look to the open space further north," said Chan. I focused on a row of tents, groups of men drilling on an open field, an array of field artillery, and Gatling guns.

"It looks like an army." I said.

"It is the California Militia. The officers are ex-Confederates."

We were skimming along a few hundred yards offshore. Chan gave an order, the boat rounded up, and the crew put nets overboard. To any onlooker, we were no different from a hundred other fishing boats on the bay. We were closer now. I again focused the telescope on the drill field. The smartly-uniformed men carrying Winchester repeaters at port arms leaped into view. They were crisp, disciplined, and drawn up in formation. At the crack of noon, a puff of smoke rose from a field gun, and in a moment, we heard the *boom!* Several carriages dashed onto the field and a half-dozen men alighted. An officer in a grey uniform saluted the civilians. They marched across the field and inspected the troops. I twisted the lens but could not make out the faces of the men.

"Who are they?" I asked.

"Leland Stanford, Charles Crocker, Mark Hopkins, and a Russian envoy," said Chan. I twisted the tubing and brought the flag waving from a tall pole into focus. It was not the stars and stripes of the United States, but a peculiar flag with a walking bear above a red stripe. In the top left-hand corner were three stars.

"What a strange flag," said I. Chan took the telescope.

"It is the bear flag, the original State of California flag, but it has three stars instead of one," said Chan.

"Three stars? But there is only one state." I said.

"They plan to annex more land," said Chan.

"Who is the Russian envoy?" I asked.

"A big handsome fellow, arrived here a couple of weeks ago and immediately went to the Russian warship," said Chan.

"Could it be a Count Borovsky?" I asked.

"Yes, that is his name. He brought papers and maps to Stanford."

"Did you say Union Iron Works?" I asked.

"Yes, the company smelts iron and manufactures mining and railroad equipment," said Chan.

"The Russian, Borovsky, knows the location of molybdenum for making a super-strong, steel alloy that could enhance the railroad industry and result in great wealth and power for its owners and overseers," said I, recalling the words of Professor Marcy.

"Aah, this Borovsky will trade the secret of the molybdenum to Stanford," said Chan.

"What does Borovsky get?" I asked.

"He wants Alaska for Russia," said Chan.

"Impossible. The Americans will never return Alaska."

"The Russians may retake it by force," Chan replied.

I again inspected the iron works with the telescope and made out what appeared to be a partially-collapsed balloon almost hidden behind a high fence.

"Can we get any closer?" I asked.

The men pulled in their nets and sculled the boat until we were no more than a hundred yards offshore. Guards ran down to the beach with rifles at port arms and waved us away. Our Chinese sailors calmly re-set their nets and ignored the armed men. The guards faltered, apparently unwilling to shoot, eventually turned their backs, and marched towards the fence. At the same time, the civilian dignitaries, with a group of officers, approached the fenced-in area.

"Stay low, keep out of sight," hissed Johnny. I stretched out on my belly and watched as the balloon took shape. It was, apparently, a demonstration for the visitors. I focused the telescope and noted heavy ropes dangling from the balloon. As the tethered balloon rose in the air, I noted something dangling from the ropes. Cautiously, I raised my camera between two burlap sacks filled with fish and snapped a series of photos.

"That's enough." Johnny Chan spoke in rapid Chinese, and soon we were off, sailing back to the Alameda shore.

From the upper deck of the returning ferry leaving Alameda, I carefully scrutinized the Russian steam frigate, the *Chesma*. She carried an impressive array of breech-loading guns mounted on modern turrets. Sailors in white shirts with horizontal blue strips polished brass and worked on the big guns. *Were they on a wartime footing?* I wondered.

Back at the hotel, I had a lemon squash and looked through the newspapers. Ian Blake had written an article when the *Chesma* arrived in San Francisco on a 'courtesy call.' She was a part of the Siberian Flotilla out of Vladivostock.

3 July 1883

I spent this morning in a darkened closet developing the gelatin plates. They were still drying when, at noon, I went out for a bite to eat. Ian Blake nursed a glass of whisky at the hotel bar. I took the next seat.

"What is a 'courtesy call'?" I asked.

"The Russian ship?"

"Yes, a Russian warship and a vicious killer named Borovsky who claims to be an envoy from the tsar. It can't be a coincidence," I said. Blake shrugged his shoulders as if my question was of no importance. *Ding*; a low chime rang from Blake's vest pocket. He withdrew a gold repeater and snapped open the case.

"What a beautiful watch. May I see it?" I asked. Without thinking or waiting for his answer, I lifted the watch from his hand. "Oh, I am sorry, but what is this?" The inscription read, *From the 1st King George's Own Gurkha Rifles to Major Ian Blake, Marchess of Brecon.*

I stared at the glowing, gold inscription for almost a minute. "You are not an impecunious poet." Blake sighed deeply, tossed down the rest of his whisky, and took the watch out of my hand.

"Why did you leave the army to be a newspaper scribbler?" I asked.

"I had a fling with the colonel's lady." He toyed with the watch and called for another drink. "I was at loose ends, heard about the Secret Service, and offered my services. Colonel Beachy-Edwards assigned me to this godforsaken post."

"With a title, you should get along well with Lady Walshingham," said I, wishing I could take it back as soon as I said it, since it sounded a bit petty. Did I really want that to happen?

"Penelope and I are old friends," Blake said.

"Damn! Am I always the last to learn these things? I should be home practicing medicine. Instead, I came on this goose chase, have been shot at, had my neck twisted and snapped, and nearly lost my life.

Instead of explaining about Penelope he said there would be a meeting with Holmes. "Shall we say, ten o'clock?" asked Blake. "I promise to reveal more then."

Penelope arrived at Dr. Bell's room within minutes of Blake. Dr. Bell had laid out a cold repast with several bottles of a local wine. She immediately went into the bathroom, slammed the door, and didn't emerge until nearly half an hour later. Penelope has shed her disguise, the padding was gone and in place of the solemn grey dress, she wore a long, red Chinese skirt, slit halfway up her leg and embellished with a formidable dragon. She posed, Turkish cigarette in hand. "A gift from Johnny Chan," she said. My heart leaped. She was as lovely as ever and I wondered, in that moment, what I could do to win her heart. It was Ian Blake, however, who, without hesitation, gallantly rose and greeted her with a kiss.

"My darling, you are absolutely ravishing," He said. Penelope practically wilted in his arms. It is amazing what a title will do for a man.

Holmes blew a cloud of smoke. "It is time for business. Mr. Blake, tell us of your observations." Blake removed a sheaf of papers from his coat pocket.

"In a nutshell, the British Empire is overextended. Mr. Gladstone has wars in Egypt and the Sudan. We are bogged down in Afghanistan and India; the Royal Navy is busy protecting the Suez Canal," Blake said.

"The American Army is almost non-existent since the end of the Indian wars," Dr. Bell added.

"That is correct. Here in California, the militia is better armed than the Army, and the officers are experienced ex-Confederates. It is the only military force on the Pacific coast," said Blake.

Holmes gestured at Blake with his pipe. "British Columbia refuses to join the Canadian Confederation until it is joined by rail with the east, but the Trans-Canada Railroad is bogged down in politics and opposition from the Indians in Alberta. Could the California Militia take British Columbia by force?"

"Yes, of course. Western Canada is a wilderness with no vestige of the British Army, but if the militia attacked, it would appear to be an invasion by the United States, and neither the Yankees nor the British want an international war," said Blake.

Penelope rose from her chair and stalked across the room. "Will you men listen to me?" she asked.

"My dear, if you have anything to add, please speak up," Holmes said.

"Yesterday, three men, probably Russians or members of the militia abducted young Leland. The old man, for all his wealth is under their control." said Penelope. The room went silent. Blake poured a glass of single malt for himself and another for Penelope.

"Great God, that is terrible, these are dangerous men. Something evil is afoot," exclaimed Holmes

"Is it my turn?" I asked.

"If you have more information, spit it out," said Blake.

I recounted my trip with Johnny Chan what I had seen of the military and the huge balloon at the iron works. I placed three photographs on table. Blake and Holmes to see my work.

"Strange, there is no gas burner. It is a not hot air balloon. Aha, this tube must lead to a tank of compressed hydrogen," said Holmes. Dr. Bell withdrew his hand lens from his vest pocket and spent several minutes going over every inch of the photo. "The balloon appears to be lifting a section of railroad track," said he.

Blake took the hand lens and peered intently at the photo. "The iron rails are pre-spiked to the wooden cross ties."

"But to what purpose?" I asked.

"Hydrogen balloons have incredible power. A balloon this size can easily lift a section of railway track and move it over difficult terrain."

Blake clapped a hand to his head. "Of course! Stanford plans to build a railroad through British Columbia to the mines in the Yukon!" said he.

Holmes stretched out his long legs, and folded his hands over his chest in the very pose I had seen so often when he solved difficult diagnostic problems.

"Mr. Stanford and his associates have extensive industrial works. A railroad through British Columbia to the Yukon would give them a monopoly on molybdenum. They would be the world's foremost manufacturer of locomotives, ships, and munitions. They would be incredibly powerful," Dr. Bell said.

"Bah! The British government would never allow a foreign company to build a railroad on their territory. It would mean war with the United States," I said.

Penelope went to the middle of the room and assumed a provocative pose, with her hand on one hip, but she was dead serious. "War is a distant problem. At this moment, I am more concerned about young Leland Stanford. He is a good boy, an only child, and the apple of his father's eye. The old man is ill. Borovsky must be the brains behind his abduction."

"Penelope is correct, but we must have more information before we can act," said Blake.

"Borovsky is scheming on behalf of Russia, but he may be taking advantage of Stanford to gain power and enrich himself. "It is late; we must have our wits about us tomorrow if we are to stop a major international conflict. We have no time to lose," Holmes said.

I could not sleep, so have resumed writing my diary with the question; How can a frozen land, so far to the north, affect the world? What can I do?

The picture of the twins, their gossamer butterfly-like costume flashed into my mind — and then death before my very eyes. Manfredi's brains splashing on the floor, the Cossack dagger in poor Codlington, and the harpoon tip that killed Dawson. I have a developed a personal grudge against Borovsky.

4 July 1883, San Francisco

At the break of day, gunfire, a band playing "Dixie," raucous shouts, drums, and trumpets woke me from sound sleep. Out on the streets, marching men carried banners and fired pistols, boys lit firecrackers under tin cans. It was the usual national exuberance when our ex-colonies celebrated their independence from Britain. Holmes and Dr. Bell were at breakfast, ignoring the sounds of bedlam from the streets. I scarcely had dressed and consumed a cup of coffee when Ian Blake burst into our rooms. He paused, breathless, and waved the San Francisco Chronicle in the air. "Read this!" Great black headlines covered the front page.

CONFEDERATE STATES OF THE PACIFIC!
A NEW COUNTRY

CALIFORNIA HAS JOINED WITH THE OREGON TERRITORIES AND SOON BRITISH COLUMBIA WILL BE A PART OF OUR MAGNIFICENT NEW COUNTRY.
LELAND STANFORD, FIRST PRESIDENT OF OUR GREAT REPUBLIC, ANNOUNCES PLANS FOR ELECTIONS

Holmes tore the paper from my hands and read the next page out loud. It was a statement by Major General Buford T. Forrest, commander of the California Militia and late of the Confederate Army. "The California Militia is now the Army of the Confederate States of the Pacific. All able-bodied men, including members of the United States Army, are invited to join our glorious cause. The pay is fifty dollars per month, three meals a day, uniform and rifle, comfortable barracks." The next page was even more ominous.

RUSSIA FIRST TO RECOGNIZE THE CONFEDERATE STATES OF THE PACIFIC

Holmes tossed the paper to the floor. "They are losing no time. Nothing can stop an invasion of British Columbia."

Blake passed back and forth until he was breathless with indignation. "They have taken the United States Mint and have plans to issue their own money. The militia is forcing Chinese men into transport ships. They will be slaves for the new country and forced to work on the railroad in British Columbia."

We were all in an uproar, outdoing one another with indignant cries and suggestions for action. Sherlock Holmes alone, kept his head and offered a sensible idea. "There isn't a moment to lose. First, we need to free young Leland Stanford. Then, his father can act sensibly," Holmes said.

"I shall contact Johnny Chan," said Blake.

While waiting for Blake's return and further word, I went out for some fresh air to clear my head and immediately encountered soldiers herding long lines of Chinese men towards the waterfront. Armed guards prevented me from walking up Nob Hill, and messengers, smartly attired in grey uniforms, dashed about on horseback. Everything pointed towards war.

While we waited for word from Blake, our afternoon tea was a dismal affair. Dr. Bell appeared to be completely without spirit. "The best we can do is contact Colonel Beachy-Edwards and request naval support," he said.

"There isn't a British ship within a thousand miles, and how could the colonel contact a ship at sea?" asked Penelope.

"She is right. Perhaps the British could organize resistance at Vancouver," said I.

"There is only a small garrison. The Russian warship will subdue resistance with a massive bombardment," Bell said.

Ian Blake, more than a bit disheveled and completely out of breath, came through the door with a rush. "Johnny Chan has a plan to rescue young Leland and do some damage to their army. Chin Ten Sing's men stole three hundred Snider-Martini rifles from the British army in Hongkong and smuggled them into Chinatown."

"What use would old-fashioned, single-shot rifles be against repeating Winchesters?" I asked. Blake bared his teeth and grinned.

"Those old British Sniders will kill a man up to fifteen hundred yards and are deadly accurate to four hundred yards. The Winchesters fire a .44 caliber bullet that is only useful at a short range."

The events from the early morning of the fifth of July until now are blurred through the lens of danger, pain, and near death. We survived an ordeal rarely experienced by human beings mostly through the ingenuity and courage of Sherlock Holmes. The following is a narrative of the events of the last few days to the best of my memory. Dr. Bell stayed in our rooms to intercept messages while the rest of us were off on our mission of mercy.

Johnny Chan and Chin Ten Sing organized the diversions that allowed us to rescue young Leland Stanford from prison. I thought it was too dangerous for Penelope, but she insisted on joining us. "The boy will trust me and no one else," she said.

Just after midnight, early on the fifth of July, girls from the house of Madame Ah Toy descended on the main gate to the military compound. The undisciplined guards opened the gates, and in the ensuing melee, more soldiers arrived from all over the compound, in varying stages of undress, thinking they were about to enjoy the pleasures of oriental lust. Instead, a dozen hatchet-wielding members of Chin Ten Sing's triad slashed at the soldiers' arms, legs, and exposed private parts. At the same time, Pow Chan and some twenty boys made their way through the fence, set fire to the officer's barracks, and set off many strings of firecrackers.

Under a light fog, Johnny Chan, with the three of us in tow, stealthily approached Hunters Point in a small sampan. The largest and most heavily armed of Chin Ten Sing's junks followed us down the bay. We lay crouched on bundles of rags and watched the frenzied activities in the industrial area. Under the glare of Edison electric lights, men fastened ropes tethering the giant hydrogen balloons to sections of railroad. The balloons rose, lifting the sections of rail to a height of twenty feet or more, while men leading horses attached to lines walked the rails to a ship. Once the balloon was in position over the ship, workers released hydrogen, allowing the balloon to lower the rails into the holds. It was an impressive display of industrial might and ingenuity. Our sampan, drifting with the current, silently approached the beach. When the shouts of soldiers and the sounds of Pow Chan's firecrackers reached our ears, a barrage of gunfire roared from the junk and extinguished the electric lights that had illuminated the shipyard. This was followed by an immense blast from the sampan's giant brass cannon. The shell exploded directly over the ship that was loading railroad tracks. One of the hydrogen balloons erupted in a great wall of flame. The Chinese fisherman sculled us close to the beach. Unfortunately, I lost my cane/pistol when I assisted Penelope over the side of the boat. Johnny Chan led us through the compound, past a giant locomotive and factories, and to the fence surrounding the military compound, which was guarded at intervals by armed sentries.

"Wait here." Chan wriggled away. There was the sound of a brief struggle. Chan returned with a large shears and severed the lowest fence wires. "The stockade holding prisoners and young Leland Stanford is straight ahead, but surrounded by another fence," he whispered. We crawled, faces in the dirt, to the stockade fence. Chan silently garroted another guard, and after waiting for a cloud to cover the moon, he clipped the wire of the second fence just enough for us to wriggle through. Chan led, I was second, followed by Penelope, and Holmes. We came to the back wall of a small, brick building, a makeshift jail. I followed Chan as he crept towards two men who guarded the front entrance. Holmes and Penelope kept well back in the shadows.

"Damn," Penelope uttered softly, when we were some twenty feet away.

"Who's there?!" The guard's lit bullseye lantern caught us in the glare. Holmes's Webley revolver roared. The light went out and the guard screamed. Johnny Chan leaped forward and garroted one guard while I caught the second with a rugby tackle that knocked him senseless.

"The boy is in the second cell," said Chan. "We must move quickly." Aided by the light of a lucifer, Holmes shot the padlock off the door and Penelope swept the boy into her arms. Chan released half a dozen Chinese prisoners who ran towards the main gate, setting off new alarms. I took the boy from Penelope. The others ran towards the boat. Young Stanford was light as a feather. He clung to my shoulders and was as good as any soldier. We would have escaped unscathed but for the Edison electric searchlight that swept across the beach. Though we ducked low to avoid being seen, we were caught in its glare. A platoon of soldiers, running with their rifles at the ready, charged across the field.

"There they are! Don't let them escape!" a leader shouted. The great Chinese junk with riflemen and cannon, was enveloped in a fog bank and could not come to our aid. When the searchlight swept away for an instant, we made a run for the beach. Penelope stumbled. I reached back to pull her onward while still holding the boy, but just at the water's edge, we were again caught in the light. There was a fusillade of rifle fire. Fortunately, the bullets whistled over our heads. I stumbled at the water's edge, but Johnny Chan took the Stanford boy and — at first running, and then swimming — finally made it safely to the waiting sampan. The soldiers were on us in a second. One whacked Holmes with the butt of his rifle, another grabbed Penelope by the hair, and a third struck me with the back of his saber. It was all over. When I regained my senses, the soldiers had hobbled our legs with lengths of rope.

We were disheveled and water-soaked to the knees, but after daubing grime from her face and adjusting her riding habit, Penelope was perfectly presentable. The Inverness cape had protected Holmes' coat, vest, and cravat from dirt, and with his aristocratic features, he was as presentable as any English squire. I was a complete mess, with a ragged hole in my filthy, tweed jacket. An especially well-muscled fellow had my left arm in a hammer lock.

"Unhand my valet! Look here, young man, we are subjects of Her Majesty, Queen Victoria, and guests of President Stanford. Kindly call off these ruffians and provide us with a conveyance to our hotel." Shouted Holmes. The fuzzy-chinned lieutenant was momentarily overwhelmed and more than a little flustered by Penelope, who rewarded him with a coquettish smile.

"My apologies for the misunderstanding, sir. Men, release these prisoners," he commanded.

As the soldiers untied the rope, a group of officers appeared on the scene. One wore the blue sash, red, striped trousers and the blue jacket of a Russian officer. He wore a large shako, and his

170

right hand was tucked into his jacket. I almost laughed; it was Borovsky posing as Bonaparte.

"NO, they are state enemies! Do NOT release them!" shouted Borovsky. The guards obeyed the Napoleon imposter. We were as helpless as caged mice. With Borovsky in the lead, the platoon of soldiers, now rather more roughly than necessary, led us back to the jail and forced us into the cell recently vacated by young Leland Stanford.

Borovsky, seated on a straight-backed chair and smoking a long cigar, gestured towards Holmes and sneered at me. "You have been a great nuisance, but, dear Penelope, I should have thought you would see that I am the only man who can truly take care of you; your fortune lies with me. It is very sad. So sad. You made a mistake by shooting me, then taking my things and running away with that idiot American, Dawson. Now, I shall devise an appropriate death for all of you." A strange light came into his eyes and his face twisted into a parody of a smile. He licked his lips, closed his eyes, and started to mutter underneath his breath. "Yes, such a delicious revenge I will not want to miss."

The man was completely mad. He gestured with his cigar to Holmes "My method of administering poison to the twins was unique, was it not? The twins could have been my concubines, my dearest companions in the new world order. But, alas, under the influence of drink, I spoke too much. They had to die before Beachy-Edwards discovered my plan to retake Alaska and the Yukon Territory."

He paused to puff at his cigar. "I detested using the knife and pistol to kill those fools in Boston. It was altogether too messy and without art. You must admit that without your damn interference these local idiots would have thought Jack Dawson died by drowning or was killed by angry Chinamen."

Holmes calmly retorted, "We are British citizens and protected by the Crown. The Secret Service will hound you to the ends of the earth if you hurt a hair of our heads.

"That is so. I could arrange to have you executed by a firing squad or by hanging, but the press, even in this new nation, would report your death to the world and there would be embarrassing questions," said Borovsky.

Penelope bit her lip, and though I would have sworn I saw fear in her eyes — and, perhaps, even tears — she was resolute in her response to his diabolical tirade. "These ruffians captured us. I shot you, but it was only a flesh wound when I could have killed you. You know I followed Dawson simply to protect the case he stole from you. How dare you ruin my cover or even question that I would betray you?! You are the one who is not loyal. If you were true to me, the Queen would surely reward you for our safe return and give me my well-deserved half. Me betray you? Ha! You have betrayed me!" said Penelope.

"Is this a tantrum? Words, words, words. A paltry reward is nothing compared to the riches of the gold and mineral wealth of the Yukon. I shall use this new nation to restore Alaska to Russia." Borovsky made another twisted smile. "I may rule Alaska myself and make the greatest fortune ever seen," he said.

The sky was lighter towards the east. It promised to be a clear day, perhaps our last. Borovsky swaggered away. The guard brought us bitter coffee, bread, and cold eggs. Within an hour, the mad Russian returned.

"The Americans agree. We will not put you to death, but give you the freedom of the sky," said he. "If you happen to have an accident while on the ride, oh well, then. . . No one can blame anyone but you for what will appear to be your incompetence at flying. Who has the power now? Ha! Da svidahnia, my British friends!"

The guards led us to a clearing where a large balloon was tethered to posts driven into the ground. Ropes suspended from the giant balloon led to a large wicker basket with a wooden floor, covered with a thick carpet. The guards hoisted us into the basket. The rascals kept Penelope in their clutches far longer than necessary. She offered them nothing but a steely gaze.

"This is an observation balloon so the surveyors can see far ahead and plot our route through the wilderness," said Borovsky.

Holmes carefully inspected the well-constructed basket. It was more comfortable than usual, presumably because the surveyors would be aloft for long periods of time. Ropes held the basket to the balloon, and a curious tube led from the balloon to the basket. The balloon itself was made of impermeable, waxed silk.

"How do we release gas in order to descend?" Bell asked.

"Very simple. Merely open this valve at the end of the tube. The wind will waft you over the mountains to the east. There you can descend and will no longer be of concern to us," Borovsky said.

Indeed, when the tethering ropes were released, we quickly ascended with a gentle, onshore breeze that swept us over the bay. Within half an hour we were over Alameda and flying towards the distant mountains. We were far higher than my one experience in a hot air balloon during our last American visit. People and houses below were mere dots. Though that last trip had at least started off pleasantly, with amazing views, this one felt much more ominous from the outset.

"I can't catch my breath," said Penelope. Holmes took in deep breaths and I was sighing more than usual.

"The atmosphere is growing rarified. I can scarcely breathe. Arthur, please open the valve," said Holmes I twisted the valve, a simple stop cock, but there was no egress of gas.

"What is wrong? We must descend immediately," said Holmes. I looked upwards, following the black tubing with my gaze. There, at its junction with the balloon was a second valve — closed. The fiend, Borovsky, had sent us aloft with no means to release gas. The incredible lifting power of hydrogen would take us high into the atmosphere, where we would die for lack of oxygen.

"We must release the gas," said Holmes. I thought of my stiletto, still strapped inside my stocking against my leg. The blade was four inches in length, attached to a wooden handle.

"I could throw the knife and perforate the bag," said I.

"No, if the blade does not strike and penetrate the balloon, we will be lost," said he.

There was only one alternative. I placed the knife in a coat pocket, grasped two of the ropes that connected us to the balloon and wrapped my legs around them, hoisting myself to the edge of the basket. I hung on to the ropes with both hands for dear life. The effort of climbing nearly took all my strength. My head began to pound for lack of oxygen. I was forced to rest after every painful attempt to climb towards the balloon, which rose rapidly, forced by skyward gusts of wind rising from the foothills. I almost lost my grasp when the basket whirled in the changing winds, but I summoned a burst of energy and made it to within an arm's length of the balloon. I made sure to wrap my legs tightly about the ropes and, with what seemed like my last ounce of strength, clung with one hand while I groped in my pocket for the knife. I grasped the handle, lifted my arm, and succeeded in stabbing a small hole in the waxed silk. There was a slight hiss of escaping gas. I slashed at it again to increase the size of the hole, but my arm was seized with a terrible cramp. The knife slipped from my useless hand and spun out of sight towards the distant earth. I may have lost consciousness for a moment, but revived enough to descend to the basket. Penelope was on the floor, lying on her side, gasping for air. Holmes sucked in great quantities of the thin air, but his lips were blue. I remained upright, but sagged against the side of the basket. The world went black and fuzzy.

It must have been mid-afternoon when I awoke. We were again over the bay. Nob Hill and the city sparkled in bright sunshine a mile or two off to the northwest. The shifting wind had first carried us south, and now, a brisk east wind pushed us over the peninsula. We had lost altitude. Holmes, with his head lolling on his shoulder, was still blue about the lips. Penelope stirred and made small mewling sounds. As I thought of our possible deaths, a great black cloud — part despair and part grief — descended on my mind. It was one of the worst moments of my life. The wind shifted and came from the south with increasing force, carrying us to the north end of the bay over the Golden Gate. We dropped, perhaps another few hundred feet. Holmes showed signs of life. I grasped his shoulder and shook his inert body until he opened his unfocused, dull eyes. I continued rubbing his arms and speaking to him until his cheeks lost their bluish hue and the old twinkle returned to his eyes. I breathed a great sigh of relief.

Penelope sat upright, rubbed her glassy eyes, and smoothed her hair. When his breathing returned to normal, Holmes peered over the side. The wind switched to the east and blew with increasing strength. "Arthur, the wind will blow us out over the sea. Borovsky fully expected us to die from asphyxiation and be blown out over the Pacific so we would be lost forever."

My elation at the possibility of descent over land evaporated. The thought of being blown over the trackless ocean filled me with despair. Our rate of descent was very slow, possibly because hydrogen, being lighter than air, escaped out the bottom of the balloon very slowly. We were at an elevation of a thousand or more feet and drifting out to sea. We watched the sun creep closer to the horizon as the fishing boats and land disappeared from sight. When the sun was a red-purple line just above the horizon, the rising wind pushed us ever more rapidly over the endless Pacific Ocean. We were low enough to make out individual white-capped waves but seemed doomed to die somewhere on that vast, trackless ocean.

At that moment, I spied jagged rocks, resembling the teeth of a saw, rising from the ocean. "Look, islands!" I shouted.

"The Farallones," said Holmes.

"It is no use. Our present course will take us beyond the islands," said I. We gazed longingly at the sheer rocky peaks and one small beach, but we were being whirled along by the wind at an altitude of at least one hundred and fifty feet. The Farallones were home to a huge colony of sea birds; gulls, terns, and gannets swooped around our balloon then dove into the sea. *If only we had the freedom of birds we could descend near the island*, I thought.

"Well now, when all seems lost, there is one consolation," said Holmes. He removed a silver flask from an inner pocket. "The water of life. Double-distilled, single malt whisky from the Isle of Skye," said he.

I was struck with a wild idea, and there was nothing to lose. "Whisky is inflammable and may be our salvation." I took the fine silver flask from his hand.

"Penelope, a bit of cloth from your blouse," said I. The dear girl immediately tore a strip of cloth which I soaked in the whisky, formed into a wick, and placed in the mouth of the flask. "I propose to light the wick and hurl it at the balloon, igniting the hydrogen," said I.

"Oh God, no! Are you crazy? The explosion will kill us!" cried Penelope.

"There is a slim chance that the force of the explosion and flames will rise. If we crouch beneath my cloak, we may, with luck, survive the burst and sudden descent," said Holmes. The fuse ignited with a small, blue flame at the strike of a second match. Penelope and Holmes crouched beneath his Inverness cloak on the floor of the basket. I gauged the distance and, with all my strength, hurled the flask with its small flame towards the rent in the balloon. Thankfully, my aim was perfect. A yellow flame flickered, and for a moment, I thought the wind had extinguished our only hope. The yellow flame climbed from the rent up the side of the balloon. I shut my eyes, but the giant ball of fire seared red through my eyelids. A shock wave and a blast of heat struck my face. Our basket swayed wildly and commenced to fall. I could not help but open my eyes to look aloft. Three ropes were still attached to a remnant of smoldering silk that acted as a giant umbrella, slowing our descent. The landing on tossing waves nearly knocked me senseless. I fell on Penelope who was curled in a fetal ball. Her forehead was bruised. Holmes was crumpled in a heap, but had sustained no serious injury.

All that kept us afloat was the wooden floor of the basket. We bobbed on the waves like a cork. Our elation at the safe landing soon turned to despair when strong currents carried us beyond the islands. When the sun disappeared beneath the horizon, it appeared we were headed to a watery death on the open Pacific. Worse, the basket was sinking into the icy cold water. The water was above our ankles, and then the numbing cold rose to our knees. Penelope became violently ill from the basket's motion and would have sunk into the water had I not used remnants of rope to lash her upright in the basket. The dreadful night wore on; patches of fog gave way to moonlight and then incredible darkness. The water was above our knees. The numbing cold was our greatest danger. Penelope's face felt like ice. Sherlock Holmes kept moving about the basket and urged us to cluster together for warmth but my mind went blank.

I thought it was a star, perhaps a shooting star coming to earth, but it was a strange flame, out of place. What was a flame doing in the midst of the Pacific? Where was I? What was happening? I scarcely felt the incredible strength of the arm that pulled me up, out of the basket over the side of a small boat, and then the bliss of stretching out on dry sacking. I was vaguely aware of Penelope and Holmes on the bottom of the boat. Sometime during that dreadful night, I was awake long enough to see an oil lantern at the very bow of the boat. The flame attracted fish, and a black bird with a noose around his long skinny neck dove into the water. In a moment, the bird surfaced with a fish clamped in its beak. An incredibly huge Chinaman took the fish and tossed it into a wooden box. It was a strange sight.

Sometime later, warm rays of sunshine warmed my numb limbs. I was desperately thirsty. My voice was a hoarse croak. "Water, do you have water?" I asked. The giant Chinaman paid no heed. I grasped his hand and pointed to my mouth. "We must have water." The fisherman opened his mouth. He had no tongue. He then pointed to his ears and shook his head. I finally understood. He was deaf and dumb. Again, I made motions of drinking. He grinned and produced a bottle of cold tea. I have never had such a wonderful drink.

Over the next hour, first Holmes then Penelope came awake and took sips of tea. When the sun was a quarter way up, the man tossed another fish into a box, raised his sail, and turned the bow of our small boat east. The onshore wind sped us along until we ran into a fog bank. The wind dropped, and for several hours, we tossed on lonely waves. The wind picked up, and by mid-afternoon, land rose out of the mists. At dusk, we skimmed through the Golden Gate and, at last, came alongside the largest of the junks that belonged to Chin Ten Sing.

I climbed the ladder and, to my pleasant surprise, Johnny Chan extended a helping hand. and the giant Chinese fisherman carried Penelope with great gentleness.

"You met Big Chan," said Johnny.

"He saved our lives," said I.

"Our enemies cut out his tongue and drove chopsticks into both ears. He is Chin Ten Sing's most faithful nephew." I winced at hearing of this horror. How could people be so inhumane?

Johnny led us to the main cabin, a great, wood-lined room hung with crimson drapes and lit with oil lanterns. We told our story while consuming huge portions of fried prawns, pork in a sweet and sour sauce, and crisp duck, all washed down with copious amounts of tea and rice brandy. Near the end of the meal, Ian Blake arrived, accompanied by Chin Ten Sing and Lotus Blossom.

"Bring us up to date. First, what happened to young Leland Stanford?" I asked, after sharing about our wretched experience.

"The boy is perfectly safe at the house of Madame Ah Toy. His father knows he is safe. Unfortunately, Mr. Stanford is still in the clutches of Borovsky," said Blake.

"They plan to remove him to the Russian ship and take him along on the invasion of British Columbia," said Johnny Chan.

"We must stop them," said Holmes.

"How? We have no money to buy off their men, no effective military force, and the Chinese laborers are at their mercy," said Blake.

"There would have been plenty of money if Chin Ten Sing could have sold the fireworks to the eastern cities for the July celebration," said Lotus Blossom.

"Why couldn't he sell fireworks?" I asked.

"A landslide blocked the railroad," Lotus Blossom replied.

Chin Ten Sing sucked in his breath. "My Chinese rockets would have lit the skies over Chicago and New York," said he.

"Their plans are no longer a secret. Borovsky is the master mind. Stanford is the reluctant figurehead of the new country. The Confederate officers have made the militia into a well-armed military force. With the aid of Russian naval guns, they plan to overwhelm Vancouver, invade British Columbia, and start work on the railroad immediately. The Chinese slave laborers will clear the way, and with the aid of hydrogen balloons, construction will move forward at an incredible speed. The Chinese will then be forced to work the mines. Borovsky will have unlimited quantities of gold and molybdenum to feed an industrial empire and will be the most powerful man in the world," said Blake.

Holmes, resting on a plush divan, stretched out his long legs and folded his hands across his chest. He gazed at old Chin Ten Sing through half-lidded eyes.

"Fireworks, you say. What else do you have besides rockets?" he asked.

"Oh, very huge rockets make great *bang* in sky and firecrackers that roar like cannon and the great dragons," said Sing.

"No commander, especially a Russian, wants to lose his ship. Most Russian sailors are brave, but illiterate, superstitious peasants." said Holmes.

"Do you have an idea?" asked Blake.

"Here are my plans."

I struggled to stay awake but was overcome by exhaustion and drifted off in a deep sleep. I was unsure how much time had passed when I finally awoke, had a cup of tea, requested paper and pencil, and set about recording the last day's events.

8-9 July 1883

Overnight, the great cabin had become a veritable war room. Ian Blake, Johnny Chan, Holmes, and old Chin Ten Sing were in deep conversation, studying a map of the Bay Area. I went on deck for a breath of fresh air. Our junk was anchored next to another, while the third blocked access to the area. Chinese laborers were busily constructing a bamboo framework on a crude, wooden raft. Chin Ten Sing came on deck and, in rapid-fire Chinese, instructed the men where to place a series of firecrackers and sparklers on the bamboo.

"The great dragon," he said.

I was mystified. "What do you mean?" I asked.

"You will see when the great dragon flashes and roars in a most fearful manner," the old man said. More small sampans and fishing boats came to the sides of our junk. Men feverishly loaded cartons and boxes onto their small boats. The old man directed the frantic activity with an authority that belied his frailty. By mid-afternoon, the boats were dispersed about the bay.

I returned to the cabin and listened to the plans. "We should kill as many of the bastards as possible," said Johnny Chan.

"Our aim is to frighten, not harm. We must persuade the captain of the Russian ship to give up and to convince the militia to stand down." said Holmes.

"They have stowed their Gatling guns and light artillery on the ship, and their army is a rabble of miners and laborers. They will break and run," said Ian Blake.

"Arthur, do you feel you have sufficiently recovered to take on a special mission? We need a strong swimmer. Are you game?" Holmes asked.

"I will do anything to get revenge on Borovsky," I said.

Holmes explained the dangerous, desperate mission.

"I will take Big Chan." said I.

"My cousin will be proud to accompany you," said Johnny Chan.

The first rocket burst over Hunters Point at midnight. More followed until the intensity and glare appeared to be a fierce artillery barrage. Ian Blake, along with hand-picked Chinese sharpshooters on a boat just off the beach, opened fire with ancient Martini rifles. Bullets punctured the two great balloons that were moored in the shipyard. A single, well-aimed rocket ignited the hydrogen, sending great balls of flame into the night sky. Johnny Chan, with his hatchet-wielding tong members, broke through the outer fence at the same time that Lotus Blossom led her ragged gang with clashing cymbals and strings of giant firecrackers. The hundreds of shouting Chinese swarmed over the encampment, sending soldiers, still dressed in their underwear, fleeing for their lives.

The waters of the bay were pitch black. I shivered in the bow of a small sampan while Big Chan sculled our boat to within a hundred yards of the Russian frigate. We quietly dropped anchor and slipped into the water. I clung to a plank and paddled with one arm while Big Chan, with powerful strokes, propelled us towards the ship. At the first crack of a rocket over the Russian ship, I raised my hand. We remained motionless, and — we hoped — out of sight, as more and more rockets exploded over, on, and near the Russians. Sailors manned the big guns but had no target and did not fire. We were close enough to dimly make out a barge propelled by a single man, which came alongside the ship until the bamboo framework practically hung over the deck. A spluttering fuse ignited hundreds of multi-colored firecrackers and sparklers that outlined a green, writhing dragon with a wicked red tongue. Immediately, the red sparklers replaced the green, outlining an even more fearsome dragon that swung a great tail at the very edge of the ship. The noise grew deafening, and in the light of the rockets, Russian sailors began jumping over the sides of the ship.

I motioned again, and Big Chan resumed paddling. I grasped the ten-inch anchor line with one hand and sawed the fibers with a long, razor-sharp knife. When Big Chan understood, he took the knife and, with one giant slash, severed the big ship's anchor line. The ship drifted with the incoming tide until bells sounded an alarm. By then, the ship went aground on a sand bar. We swam back to our small boat in time to see Pow Chan and dozens of his young lads swarm over the side of the Orient and Pacific steamer that held Chinese laborers in locked cages below deck. They quickly subdued the guards and hacked open the cages. Chinese laborers fled the ship and joined the mob to overcome the soldiers.

It was all over by morning. Holmes and I, in the comfort of the great cabin, sipped tea and listened to the latest incoming reports. For the lack of clean, dry clothing, Chin Ten Sing had supplied us with silk pajamas and long robes, which were surprisingly comfortable. The Army of the Confederate States of the Pacific was a disorganized rabble. General Forrest and his California Militia officers fled inland. According to rumor, they went to the Yosemite land grant where it is said that thousands of men could live and hide for years and never be discovered. Penelope, in a stunning, long, slit skirt supplied by Lotus Blossom, collected young Leland Stanford from the comforts of Madam Ah Toy's House of Pleasure and returned him to Mr. Stanford, who immediately renounced the new country and pledged renewed allegiance to the United States.

There was a small sensation when, wearing our Chinese clothing and carried in sedan chairs, Holmes and I arrived at our hotel. Long, hot baths, bacon, eggs, and coffee, provided by Dr. Bell restored my spirits and re-energized my aching body. Dr. Bell blew a long, contemplative cloud of smoke towards the ceiling.

"One question remains. Where is Borovsky? We must bring him to justice," said Dr. Bell.

I accompanied Ian Blake and Johnny Chan to the shipyard and to every lodging house in the city in search of the evil Russian. Pow Chan and his boys combed the streets, but there was no sign of him. We were famished and tired by the search. We ended the day together with dinner at the Restaurante Italiano on the waterfront. Other than the missing Russian, the news was fairly good. The inscrutable Lam Qua reported that the casualties among the Chinese amounted to only a few split heads and no deaths. While fishing boats came to the dock, I toyed with noodles and shrimp in tomato sauce and a glass of red wine.

Two steam tugs, with cables attached to the bow, managed to pull the Russian ship off the sandbar and tow it towards the Golden Gate. The ship came opposite the restaurant, and before our eyes, a figure wearing a blue coat and carrying a revolver backed away from the forward gun turret. His head was bald as a cue ball. A half-dozen cutlass-wielding sailors slowly advanced, under the command of an officer.

"There, there on the ship! It's Borovsky!" I shouted.

"I have a rifle in the cab. One shot would bring him down," said Blake.

"Under our law, he is innocent until a jury pronounces him guilty. An American court would dither over who has jurisdiction, and it would take months to bring him up before a British Court." said Dr. Bell. Lam Qua made an enigmatic smile and nodded agreement.

"You will remember my successful treatment of the tsar's son in Russia two years ago?" asked Dr. Bell.

"That I do, but what does that have to do with Borovsky?" I asked.

Dr. Bell blew a great cloud of smoke. "A word to the tsar about Borovsky's perfidy will bring the man to a Russian dungeon and then execution in cold blood," he said.

"Ah, you are a very clever man," said Johnny Chan.

We heard a faint shout; the Russian sailors made a dash towards Borovsky, who fired a single shot. The sailors backed off until, again, the officer goaded them forward.

"The Russians must have found him out," said Bell, as he gestured towards the ruckus.

Quick as a cat, Borovsky leaped on to a hawser that connected to a port side tugboat and went, hand over hand, to the tug's deck. A great bank of fog rolled over the bay, and in an instant, we lost sight of the tug and its evil passenger.

10 July 1883

We were at dinner this evening when a tired Johnny Chan joined us. "We searched the city again. He has vanished into thin air," he said.

"Where is Penelope?" I asked.

"I have not seen her since, well, since yesterday," said Ian, suddenly sounding worried.

Though I know more than most how Penelope mysteriously comes and goes at her leisure, this is different. Something is not right . . .

15 July 1883

I have been in a funk, sick with worry over Penelope, these past few days. We have searched everywhere, but have not been able to find a single clue to her disappearance. Shortly after dinner tonight, a bellboy brought a folded sheet of cheap foolscap. My name was on the outside leaf.

Doyle, you can have her for a bank note of one million U. S. dollars. Come alone to the fall of fire.

Holmes sniffed the paper and examined the bit of the gum that had sealed the folded page. "The message is crudely written with what appears to be a charcoal, it smells of wood smoke, and the gum is from an incense cedar, a tree that exists only in the upper alpine strata," he said.

"Where is the fall of fire?" I asked.

"High in the mountains," replied Holmes.

Ian Blake rested his head in his hands. "The bastard has taken her to the mountains. We don't even know if she is alive," he said. He lifted his face. I saw tears in his eyes. Ian Blake was in love with Penelope. I may have felt passion or lust for the damsel, but Blake's love was genuine.

"I will get Borovsky if it is the last thing on earth I do," he said.

"Perhaps he is attempting to join the militia and go to Mexico," I said.

"We need transportation and money. Leland Stanford owes it to us," Ian said. Without wasting a moment, off we went to the home of Leland Stanford.

His study was lit by a single bulb in a lamp on his desk. Mr. Stanford was in the shadows, slumped in a chair at his desk. "Your Russian friend abducted Lady Penelope Walshingham," said Ian.

"He misled me; the man is unscrupulous. I will do everything in my power to make amends," Stanford said.

"He demands a banknote for one million dollars and we must have transportation. His is ahead of us by several days," Ian said.

"Ah, well, I owe you at least that much for the recovery of my son," Sanford sighed. He withdrew a checkbook from the desk drawer and, with a heavy hand, signed his name for a million dollars. "Now, about transportation. Where is the rascal?" he asked.

"Chinese grapevine says he is in the Yosemite wilderness," Johnny Chan said.

"That location fits with my observations of his note," said Holmes.

Leland Stanford unrolled a map of Northern California. "Here is the Yosemite Valley. A riverboat could take you to the upper end of the bay near San Jose, and then, my chief engineer will conduct you the rest of the way in his latest invention," he said.

"How long will it take?" Ian asked.

"You can be at the head of the bay by dawn, and should reach the valley by mid-morning," Stanford said.

"Impossible . . . Yosemite is more than two hundred miles away, there are few roads, and the area becomes mountainous," replied Ian. Stanford smiled for the first time.

"You will leave this very night and will travel by air," said he.

"This is more adventure than I care for. You fellows go, while I wrap up my lectures," Dr. Bell said.

We assembled warm clothing for the high altitudes, a basic medical kit, revolvers for Holmes and I, and a Martini rifle for Ian Blake. We did not forget a repast of cold salmon, a generous roast of beef with mustard, and a loaf of crisp, sourdough bread.

Just before midnight we boarded the boat and were underway on a southerly course down San Francisco Bay. Since the boat is for daytime passengers, we slept on the deck.

186

16 July 1883

"Far as we go, boys. Rise and shine!" the captain shouted. The water was shallow, and we were anchored well off the marshy shore.

I rubbed the sleep out of my eyes and became aware of slow, steady cursing that arose from the foredeck. The cook offered hot coffee with a boiled egg and a slice of bread. With these meager rations in hand, I went forward, only to become entangled in a skein of ropes and electric wires. The engineer for the balloon, a slender fellow with blond hair swore in German and English. "Da damn valve be stuck," he said. Two men worked feverishly with wrenches and hammers to free the valve that should allow hydrogen to flow from a series of tanks into a giant balloon that lay useless and collapsed on deck.

"Is that our transportation to the mountains?" I asked.

The engineer smoothed his hair, "Ya, ya, she will take you anywhere," he said.

"I have had enough of ballooning. The wind is just as likely to take us out to sea as to the Yosemite Valley," said I.

"This balloon can fly against the wind or in any direction you choose," he said. Then, I spied what appeared to be an engine with a propeller attached by braces to the basket. "The latest electric motor, from Germany, powered by lead acid batteries," the engineer said with a proud wave of his hand.

Holmes and Ian Blake paced the deck, muttering oaths. At last, just before noon, Blake seized a wrench from Adolph, the engineer and with a great heave, he moved the valve's lever a quarter turn. A bit of hydrogen hissed into the balloon. With another mighty heave, he opened the valve completely. Slowly, the balloon filled and rose from the deck. When, at last, it was high enough to lift the passenger's basket, I understood how the balloon could fly against the wind. The electric motor, with a six foot, wooden propeller, was attached by a pivot to braces that extended from the basket. A tiller-like handle extended from the motor so it could be turned in any direction. It was nearly four o'clock in the afternoon when we entered the basket; Holmes first, followed by Ian Blake, and then me, with our provisions.

"It is very simple. This switch starts the motor, using current from battery number one. When the battery runs out of electricity, we switch to battery number two and then, with this hand cranked generator, re-charge the first battery. Above all, do not disconnect a wire. A single spark could ignite the hydrogen," explained the engineer.

With those simple instructions, Adolph sat on a bench and, with tiller in hand, ordered the boat's crew to cast off the tethering lines. We ascended to about one hundred feet. Holmes, with a map and compass, ordered the course. "A point north of due east will bring us to the Merced River where it arises from the mountains," he said.

Adolph started the motor and turned the tiller until the propeller faced in the direction ordered by Holmes. The basket rotated, and we moved to the east. The engineer adjusted our height to about five hundred feet, where we found a favorable wind. With the combined force of wind and propeller, we fairly flew over the marshes and swamps that surrounded the San Francisco Bay. Soon, we were over cultivated fields and a series of rivers.

Holmes ordered course adjustments from time to time. "There, there, below us is the junction of the Merced River with the San Joaquin!" he shouted. Yes, he was correct; according to the map, the Merced from joined the San Joaquin at an almost exact right angle. We were on course; the jagged saw-toothed Sierra Nevada mountains were dead ahead, but the sun was a red glow in the west. Soon, we were in darkness, but followed the glimmering river with little trouble.

"I do not like to fly in the mountains in the dark. We must stop for the night," said Adolph.

"No, every minute counts," said Ian.

"We flew on with only the sound of the motor and the whirling propeller for company.

"Ach, I refuse to go further," Adolph cried.

"There, just ahead — a glimmer of light!" I shouted. Adolph released hydrogen until we hovered less than a hundred feet above the river. The glimmer of light was a small campfire.

"We go down here," Adolph said. He gently let us down, and when we hovered a mere five feet above a bare, grassy area, I hopped out and secured the tethering lines to boulders along the river.

We warily approached the campfire and soon spied a solitary figure sitting with his back to a huge, smooth boulder. A blackened pot stood on coals alongside the fire.

"Be ye a seekin' a spot o' tae?"

"Aye, we are, and ye hale from East Lothian," said Holmes. The fire flared up, and in its light, I made out a fellow with a flowing, white beard who wore a slouch hat and a leather vest over a flannel shirt. Adolph busied himself with securing the balloon while the three of us found places around the fire.

"You have the accent of Scotland," I said.

"Aye, I left Dunbar while I was a wee lad. I am called John Muir," said our new friend.

"I am Arthur Conan Doyle from Edinburgh. The other lads are Ian Blake and Sherlock Holmes, both Englishmen.

Would ye care for a drop o spirit in your tea?" Mr. Muir asked. We shared our provisions and had a jolly time. "What brings ye to the valley of the Yosemite?"

"What is the fall of fire?" I asked.

Mr. Muir pulled his beard and sipped tea before answering. "That would be the Horsetail Falls that flow from El Capitan. On certain evenings, just at sunset, the falling water and the spray glows as if on fire," he said.

"Will you guide us to the falls?" I asked.

"Aye, for a fellow Scots, I will do that."

17 July 1883

We slept under the stars, rose early, and after tea and a chunk of Muir's rough brown bread, we hiked towards the falls. Muir, in his kindly way, suggested we take only the necessities. "We travel light and fast," he said. We crunched over a gravel trail and jumped from one polished boulder to another alongside the Merced River. We were surrounded by tall lodge pole pines, and I spied flakes of obsidian that could have been arrow points. There were patches of summer snow in shady areas, and it grew colder as the day wore on to late afternoon. Muir insisted we stay close because grizzly bears are famous — or should I say infamous — in these parts. He pointed out plants and animal tracks as if he were a professor in nature's university.

Near evening, we came upon an open, grassy meadow with blue lupines, surrounded with towering granite ramparts. "There be the falls," said Muir. We flung ourselves down on tufts of grass in a grove of pine trees alongside the river. Every muscle ached. I was bone tired from our hike but was enlivened by the river cascading as if forever falling down, down, down from the glacial granite rocks above. It was, indeed gorgeous and majestic.

A piercing scream rent the evening air and echoed back and forth from canyon wall to wall. It had to be Penelope, but where?

"There, there on the second ledge", Blake shouted. He sprung up and was off, bounding from boulder to boulder. He stumbled and went down. At a glance, I knew he had a broken ankle. "Please, rescue her," he said.

Holmes set out across the meadow; I followed staying in the shadows while the setting sun flashed on the falling water until it appeared to be a river of golden fire. Holmes leaped to a path that ascended next to a slick granite wall. Another faint, high-pitched shout came from higher up. Holmes ran like a deer, but the path narrowed and on one side was a sheer drop into roaring water. I was fifty yards behind him, Borovsky's head popped up. He fired a pistol shot. The bullet chipped rock within a foot of Holmes's head.

"Leave the money and go or I will kill her," Borovsky shouted.

Holmes ducked out of sight while I crept closer, my back pressed against the granite wall. The million-dollar check was in a wallet, tied around my neck with a cord. The powerful force of the torrential flow of water, which was swollen by melting snow plunged from a great height. The spray rolled up like the smoke from a cathedral on fire. The narrow valley into which the river hurls itself is a huge chasm lined by wet, glistening stones; it narrowed into a ravenous pit of incalculable depth. It seemed impossible that Holmes could climb without being seen. Then, through the dying light and mists, a hundred feet higher up the trail, I glimpsed Borovsky on a ledge with his hand around Penelope's neck. At the same time, Holmes bounded up the curving path that wound upwards to a ledge at the side of the falls. I followed but just beneath the ledge, I fell on a root and nearly slipped away over the precipice. I clung to the wet rock at the edge of the trail but slipped, inch by inch, to the edge and was about to fall into the torrent. Holmes saw my predicament and his strong hand grasped mine. "They are just above us. I will go for him. You take care of Penelope," Holmes said. There was another piercing cry and sounds of a struggle just above us. Holmes found a tenuous footing on a niche in the rock face and with great effort swung up on to the ledge.

"Damn you," shouted Borovsky.

For a moment there was only the sound of blows and heavy breathing. Borovsky's pistol clattered over the brink. I climbed onto the ledge. Penelope was lying face down at next to the granite wall, seemingly out of harm's way, Borovsky had Holmes in a death grip, with an arm lock.

"Let him go! I have the money", I shouted.

The Russian released his grip long enough for Holmes to take a deep breath and land a kick on Borovsky's knee.

Borovsky pulled a long knife from a belt sheath, crouched, and with a menacing growl lunged and drove the blade deep into Holmes's chest. I watched through a haze of mist in the near darkness. Holmes coughed and spewed blood and fell on the slick granite. The mad Russian kicked Holmes motionless body. Borovsky seemed satisfied that Holmes was no longer a threat. He turned towards me and pressed the tip of the knife against my neck, close to the carotid artery. I dared not move.

"You bastard," he said. "I could have taken Alaska and been rich."

The knife went deeper into my neck. A warm stream of blood trickled down my chest. With strength fueled by anger and despair, I landed a blow on Borovsky face. He fell back; the knife fell away into the gorge. "The money, the money" he shouted.

I dodged away from one precarious hand hold to the next until I was behind the cascade of water where the narrow ledge widened to a half-dozen feet. He was on me again and crashed a great fist into my chest. I fell just at the edge and yanked at his ankles until he tumbled backwards, striking his head against the granite wall.

We rose at the same time, facing each other, laboring for breath, and soaked with water. I feinted to one side, then crouched and delivered a head butt to his solar plexus. He let out a great *wuff* of air and went down but, with his super strength, managed to grasp my right leg. I kicked, but he held fast and slid, inch by inch, over the slick rock. His kicking feet went first, then his legs, until he dangled while still holding on to me. In a second or two, I would surely have gone off the trail with him and been pulverized by the deadly rocks below. I wrapped my right hand around the stump of a gnarly tree embedded in the side of the trail and struggled and struggled, but he did release his death grip. The man had an evil strength. Within seconds, we would both plunge to our deaths.

"Hold fast, Arthur." It was Holmes. He was deathly pale and struggling to breath, but with strength that rose from his indomitable character, he had revived.

Sherlock Holmes lay at the very edge on a bit of crumbling rock. I cradled his head for a moment. There was a chance that he could survive the wound to his lung.

"Arthur, you are a dear friend and have become a remarkable man. Remember me, please."

With those last words, he leaned far over, head down and reached for Borovsky's hand that clutched my leg. There was an audible 'crack', when he fractured Borovsky's finger. The Russian plunged into the abyss, carrying Holmes with him.

Penelope's pitiable moans led me to where she lay in a pool of water in a crevice. Her ankles were tied, and a white splinter of her broken humerus bone protruded from her left arm just above her elbow. She was nearly unconscious and could barely stand. I rested for a long time, then managed to carry her down the treacherous trail. Hours later, we spotted the campfire.

Ian Blake brewed strong tea, laced with single malt whiskey. I revived quickly. By the light of a roaring fire, I washed Penelope's wound with carbolic and pulled on her arm until the bones were together under the skin. Fortunately, the medical kit had clean dressings to bind her arm.

18 July 1883

After warming myself by the fire, I fell asleep from sheer exhaustion. Ian Blake never left Penelope's side.

At dawn this morning, I went up the trail to search his body but there was no sign of Holmes. Strangely enough, even though was certain he was dead, I could not find Borovsky. I shed bitter tears. Holmes had sacrificed his life to save me and now, I could not even find his body for a decent burial.

Hours later, Adolph took us away in his marvelous balloon. Muir, as good an honest a man as ever came out of Scotland, wished us goodbye and refused our offer of compensation for his good work. Despite variable winds and a shower of rain, Adolph returned us to San Francisco before dark.

21 July 1883

Even when we had returned safely to our rooms in San Francisco, Ian refused to leave Penelope's side. She awoke sometime during that night. For a moment, I detected the old flash in her eye, but part of her spirit had vanished on that terrible ledge beneath Horsetail Falls. She gazed at Ian with a look that I had never seen. It was no surprise when she said she had decided to stay and seek her fortune in San Francisco.

I had planned to return the check to Mr. Stanford, but the ink had run on sodden paper. The check was completely worthless.

A bored fellow at the consulate took note of the death of Sherlock Holmes but the secret service took little notice.

The afternoon of the next day, Dr. Bell and I crossed the bay. Pow Chan carried our bags. Lam Qua and Johnny Chan bid us farewell when we boarded the eastbound train.

During those days of travel across the United States, I scribbled the beginning of a story about Sherlock Holmes.

15 August 1883, our last day at sea

This evening, immediately after dinner, we were idly watching for our imminent landfall. Dr. Bell, very much out of character, put an arm on my shoulder.

"Arthur, I have had enough adventuring. What are your plans?" he asked.

"I shall be happy enough to care for anemic old ladies with poor digestion and I shall preserve the memory of Sherlock Holmes" I said.

***

Editor's note:

Six months later, Leland Stanford and his family embarked on a grand tour of Europe. His only son, Leland Jr., contracted typhoid fever and died in Italy. Stanford endowed Stanford University in memory of his son.

There were no further entries in the diary. The last half-dozen pages were blank, but while we were leafing through the journal, three pages fell out from between the last page and the back cover; a one-page letter written in a lady's penmanship and what was clearly a draft of a two-page letter, which contained numerous scribbles and crossed out words. For the sake of clarity and ease of reading, we have eliminated all the errata and both are published below in a legible form.

The one-page letter:

8 April 1885

Dear Arthur,

It is such a long time since we parted. You may be surprised to know you are never far from my thoughts. I imagine you are successful in your medical practice and that your career in literature will be equally admirable. I am well. Ian discovered a cache of small arms left behind by the fleeing army/militia. He sold a number of repeating Winchester rifles and Colt revolvers to Chin Ten Sing and purchased a parcel of land in the Napa Valley. Our vineyard is not as grand as an English country estate, but we are content. Visit if you come to California again.

Kisses,
Penelope, [Lady Ian Blake]

The two-page draft letter:

Bush Villa
Southsea
1885

Dear Dr. Bell,

I hope you are quite well and in good spirits. Penelope sent word that she and Ian are happy together and enjoying life in California. Quite a change, I imagine, from international double agent to vintner, though she seems to have adjusted nicely.

Though that is news, it is not, however, the reason for my writing to you today. Rather, my intent is two-fold. First, I must thank you for all you taught me from the time you took me on as your clerk.

Indeed, you have been a most formidable figure in helping me become a doctor, and my practice is allowing me a comfortable existence. As well, you know of my life-long desire to create a more complete literary work of my own than the short story published anonymously years ago. I have made Sherlock Holmes into a consulting detective who solves many great mysteries . Although I have yet to fully flesh out the tale, I am committed to publishing it within the next two years and have even been consulted regarding its ultimate publication by Beeton's Christmas Annual.

The second reason for this missive is to share news of my impending nuptials. You know, more than most, that I have always been an imaginative sort, especially as regards adventure and romance. Though it took me until now to realize it, there's surely a difference between believing a thing and knowing it. My dear, sweet, Louisa, who is soon to be Mrs. Arthur Conan Doyle, is better than any fantasy and will become my wife in August of this year.

Yours very truly,
Arthur Conan Doyle

Also from MX Publishing

MX Publishing is the world's largest specialist Sherlock Holmes publisher, with over a hundred titles and fifty authors creating the latest in Sherlock Holmes fiction and non-fiction.

From traditional short stories and novels to travel guides and quiz books, MX Publishing caters to all Holmes fans.

The collection includes leading titles such as *Benedict Cumberbatch In Transition* and *The Norwood Author* which won the 2011 Howlett Award (Sherlock Holmes Book of the Year).

MX Publishing also has one of the largest communities of Holmes fans on Facebook with regular contributions from dozens of authors.

www.mxpublishing.com

Also from MX Publishing

"Phil Growick's, *'The Secret Journal of Dr Watson'*, is an adventure which takes place in the latter part of Holmes and Watson's lives. They are entrusted by HM Government (although not officially) and the King no less to undertake a rescue mission to save the Romanovs, Russia's Royal family, from a grisly end at the hand of the Bolsheviks. There is a wealth of detail in the story but not so much as would detract us from the enjoyment of the story. Espionage, counter-espionage, the ace of spies himself, double-agents, double-crossers . . . all these flit across the pages in a realistic and exciting way. All the characters are extremely well-drawn and Mr Growick, most importantly, does not falter with a very good ear for Holmesian dialogue indeed. Highly recommended. A five-star effort."

The Baker Street Society

The characters return in the sequel, *The Revenge of Sherlock Holmes.*

When the papal apartments are burgled in 1901, Sherlock Holmes is summoned to Rome by Pope Leo XIII. After learning from the pope that several priceless cameos that could prove compromising to the church, and perhaps determine the future of the newly unified Italy, have been stolen, Holmes is asked to recover them. In a parallel story, Michelangelo, the toast of Rome in 1501 after the unveiling of his Pieta, is tasked by Pope Alexander VI, the last of the Borgia pontiffs, with creating the cameos that will bedevil Holmes and the papacy four centuries later. For fans of Conan Doyle's immortal detective, the game is always afoot. However, the great detective has never encountered an adversary quite like the one with whom he crosses swords in "The Vatican Cameos."

"An extravagantly imagined and beautifully written Holmes story"
(Lee Child, NY Times Bestselling author, Jack Reacher series)